HOW TO TEND A GRAVE

HOW TO TEND A GRAVE

A NOVEL

JOCELYN SHIPLEY

Great Plains Teen Fiction
(an imprint of Great Plains Publications)
345-955 Portage Avenue
Winnipeg, MB R3G 0P9
www.greatplains.mb.ca

Great Plains Publications gratefully acknowledges the financial support provided for its publishing program by the Government of Canada through the Canada Book Fund; the Canada Council for the Arts; the Province of Manitoba through the Book Publishing Tax Credit and the Book Publisher Marketing Assistance Program; and the Manitoba Arts Council.

Design & Typography by Relish Design Studio Inc.

Printed in Canada by Friesens

Library and Archives Canada Cataloguing in Publication

Shipley, Jocelyn
How to tend a grave / Jocelyn Shipley.

Issued also in electronic formats.
ISBN 978-1-926531-19-9

I. Title.

PS8587.H563H69 2012 jC813'.6 C2011-907032-4

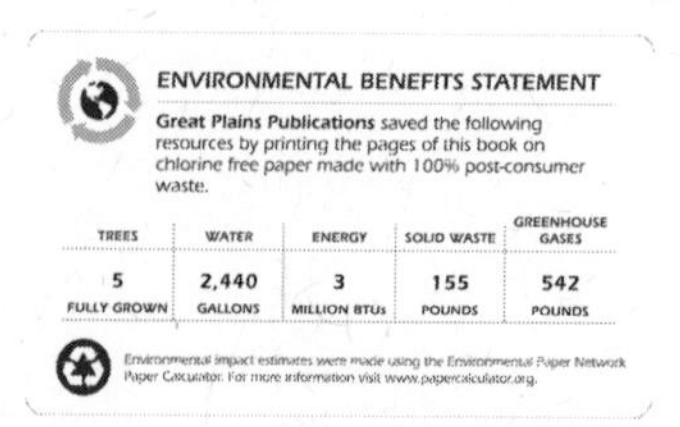
ENVIRONMENTAL BENEFITS STATEMENT

Great Plains Publications saved the following resources by printing the pages of this book on chlorine free paper made with 100% post-consumer waste.

TREES	WATER	ENERGY	SOLID WASTE	GREENHOUSE GASES
5 FULLY GROWN	2,440 GALLONS	3 MILLION BTUs	155 POUNDS	542 POUNDS

Environmental impact estimates were made using the Environmental Paper Network Paper Calculator. For more information visit www.papercalculator.org.

For my family

Dead

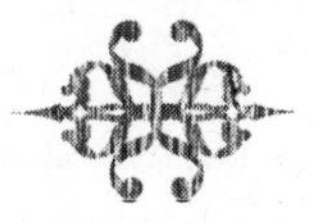

When the cops come to the door, Liam's passed out in front of the TV with his iPod on. He pulls his earbuds out and checks the time. Four a.m. What the—?

Is his mom getting busted? But she knows her Criminal Code and works within the law. Still, things happen. And why else would the cops be here?

He drags himself to the door and opens it with a dazed smile. "Hey there, officers! How can I help you this fine May morning?"

They look stunned to see him. Like maybe they were expecting a pimp or something? But it's only Liam, a groggy teen in blue striped boxers and a Save-the-Salmon T-shirt.

The cops flash IDs and introduce themselves. Liam doesn't respond. Don't engage, that's what his mom would say. Be cool. But that doesn't stop them firing questions. "Do you know a Monica Hall? Does she live here? When did you last see her?"

How'd they even get into the building? This condo is a high-security place. There's a concierge 24/7. And no matter who's on duty, those guys don't let anybody they can't identify past the lobby. But of course the cops can do whatever they want. Can and will, his mom says.

But what if they're rogue cops? Criminals in disguise? Happens on TV.

He stays tough. Be silent if you're ever interrogated, his mom's told him. Don't incriminate yourself. Never admit to anything. That's how she operates.

She calls herself an accountant, which isn't a lie. She does collect the cash and keep the books for Arabella Investments. It's not her problem if people assume that's a financial firm. What I do for a living is nobody's business but mine, she says. I pay taxes. I give to charity. I recycle. I vote. Anybody asks you anything else, you don't know.

There's two cops, one male, one female. The guy, not in uniform so he must be a detective, is paunchy and balding and chewing gum like he'd really rather be having a smoke. "I'm giving you one last chance, kid." As if Liam's a bit thick and this is a huge favour. "Do you know Monica Hall?"

Liam plays along. If you have to say something, be polite and courteous, his mom has also told him. Throw them off with an unexpected response. "I'm sorry, but Monica's not here right now." Calm and polite. "Can I take a message? Maybe have her call you tomorrow?"

Now the detective looks like he wants to smack Liam. The female cop, who is in uniform, steps forward. "Hey, hey, it's all right," she says. "We're here to help. Is Monica your big sister?" Her oh-you-poor-kid tone clues Liam in. Something's wrong with his mom.

Really, really wrong.

"She's not my sister," he says. "She's my mom. Monica Hall is my mother."

He waits while they process that. The female cop quickly hides her shock. The detective stops chewing his gum long enough to repeat Liam's words. "Your mother," he says. "You're telling us that Monica Hall is your mother?" Doesn't even try to hide his contempt.

And then it's Liam wanting to smack him.

But that would be bad. His mom's raised him to hate any kind of violence. She doesn't even approve of killing spiders or swatting flies. She catches them and sets them free outside.

"What's going on?" Panic floods his voice. "Where is she?" His left leg starts to tremble. He stomps down hard on his foot but can't make the shaking stop. "Is she okay? Please tell me she's okay."

"Can we sit?" The female cop points to the dark chocolate-brown sofa where Liam was sleeping. The big plump cushions make a squishing sound as they all sink into the vegan faux leather. His mom wanted the look without the cruelty to cows. Liam almost laughs because it sounds like they've all sat down on a huge whoopee cushion.

"I'm sorry," the female cop says, "but we have some bad news." The detective sweeps the room with his eyes.

Liam's mom spent a lot of money on a decorator over the winter, so everything is coordinated and the latest style. At least that's what she says. He wouldn't know the difference. All he cares about is the widescreen TV and the surround-sound system. But he can see the detective's wondering how they can afford to live in such an upscale condo.

Truth is they can't. They only live here because this guy his mom knows lets them. One of her regular clients. He's old and rich and in love with her. He set them up and pays for everything because he wants her to quit the game and marry him. Which she's thinking about.

But she's conflicted. She doesn't really believe he'll ever leave his wife and kids. And even if he does, why give up her freedom to be dependent on a man?

"There's been an accident," the female cop says. "A hit-and-run."

Liam picks up one of the pillows his mom had made to accessorize the sofa. She spent weeks finding the right lime and hot pink fabric, in a geometric pattern she called "sixties retro." He'd laughed at her accessorizing a sofa, like it was an outfit or something. "What's that got to do with my mom?"

The female cop sets her notebook in her lap. Reaches over to pat his shoulder, then pulls back before she actually touches him. "Monica Hall," she says. "Monica Hall, your mother. I am so, so sorry, but she was the victim." Their eyes meet and he can see she's not being fake. She really hates telling him this and is almost ready to cry herself. "I know this is going to be a terrible shock for you. But she's dead."

"What?" That can't be true. Half an hour ago it was just a normal night, with him falling asleep on their first-ever-brand-new-sofa, watching sports and listening to music. Waiting for his mom to come home.

Waiting for her to wake him up so he'd know she was okay. Then he'd have a snack and go to bed. His mom would stay up, relaxing with a glass of wine and maybe watching a movie. Then in the morning he'd go to school and she'd sleep until noon.

But this cop just told him that his mom is dead.

He stares at the vase of pink roses on the coffee table. His mom bought them fresh this morning. "How do you know it was her?"

"We found her purse and her cellphone." Then they give him a lot of details that he doesn't want to hear but has to know, like that she probably died instantly and didn't suffer, and they're looking for witnesses but don't suspect foul play, and they'll need someone to identify the body.

He sits there and hugs the pillow. His mom was so happy with that thing, and the five other pillows she ordered in coordinating fabrics. She was always at him not to spill anything on them, because they cost a hundred bucks each.

The detective strides off into the kitchen to make some calls. The female cop stays sitting there with Liam. Waiting for him to speak. But he can't.

He's always been afraid something terrible would happen to his mom. That she'd get beaten up or raped or maybe infected with HIV. But he never, ever, ever expected something like this. He never imagined his mom would be run down in the street and left lying in a pool of blood.

Dead.

He never thought his mom could *die*.

"You shouldn't be alone right now," the female cop says. "Is there somebody you can call? A relative or friend?"

"Not really." There's the guy who owns this place. But he's never actually met Liam. Not until he gets a divorce, his mom says. Liam doesn't even know the guy's real name. Just calls him Mr. Cash & Condo. And besides his wife and family, Mr. Cash & Condo has some high power Bay Street job.

He definitely won't want to be involved.

There's Laverne, his mom's business partner. But Liam doesn't really know her, either. Sure, she'll be devastated, but she'll want to stay out of this. No way will she want the cops asking her questions. She'll be keeping her head down to protect Arabella Investments.

As for friends, Liam's been careful to avoid making any. Because what if somebody found out about his mom? Say some kid came over and saw her getting ready for work? He doesn't want any teenage guys checking her out. Or judging her. Or telling their parents, or other kids, about her. So he's a loner by choice.

Too bad, because Mr. Cash & Condo gives him great tickets for Jays and Raptors and Leafs games. It would be cool to take a friend along. But he goes with his mom, or scalps the extra ticket and goes alone.

Now it hits him that he'll have to start saying *did*, or *used to*.

His mom is dead.

Life as he knew it is over.

"No other family?" The female cop rubs her temples like she has a headache or something. "There must be somebody."

So he calls Gully. His mom's father. His grandfather. Even though he hardly knows him. But Gully is his only living relative. There's nobody else.

He doesn't want to make the call with such horrible news. But if he doesn't, the cops will. He says the words like it happened to some other kid. Like he's telling Gully the plot of a movie or something.

It's not until Gully finally stops shouting no, no, no, that Liam starts blubbering. "What should I do?" he sobs. "Oh man, I don't know what to do."

"It's okay," Gully says. "I'm on my way, and it's going to be okay, trust me, it is." After he hangs up, Liam breaks down completely.

His mom is dead. Dead!

But Gully, the grandfather he barely knows, is getting in his truck and driving west. He's speeding down the 401 from Dunlane to Toronto. He's coming here to Mr. Cash & Condo's place and he's going to look after everything.

Stay

Turns out Gully's a take-charge kind of guy. True to his word, he arrives less than three hours later. He talks to the cops, identifies his daughter's body and deals with the media. Because of course Monica Hall's death makes the morning news.

A hit-and-run in downtown Toronto is an outrage! Not as sensational as if she'd been shot or stabbed, or maybe if she'd been a celebrity or a politician. But then there's the sex worker angle to exploit. Was it really an accident? Or was she murdered because of her high-risk job?

The police issue a statement saying there is no evidence to indicate that Monica Hall's death was related to her line of work. She wasn't run down by an angry client or a bad date. She was simply in the wrong place at the wrong time, killed by a drunk driver, or maybe kids street racing. They haven't yet found the car that hit her, but they will pursue all leads. They will find out who did this and prosecute them.

Gully makes a statement too: *No comment. Please respect our privacy*. Which doesn't stop the media from stalking them, phoning to beg for an interview and hanging out in front of the building trying to get past the concierge.

While he and Liam hide inside, Gully cooks a lot of food that doesn't get eaten. He deals with Mr. Cash & Condo and Liam's school. He arranges for Monica's body to be taken to

Dunlane. He calls her business partner Laverne to come over and help them sort out her stuff.

But none of them can face the pain of going through Monica's things. So Laverne keeps the best shoes, clothes and jewellery, and they donate everything else to a women's shelter. Are you sure you don't want something to remember her by? Laverne keeps asking Liam.

But what would he keep? He doesn't want any of the expensive jewellery given to his mom by her clients. How he wishes they owned just one family photo album to save.

But they don't. Still, it's not like Liam's going to forget his mom. And Gully feels the same way. He doesn't want any of his daughter's possessions. He'll just keep the memories, he says. Well, the good ones, anyway.

The next day is a blur. Liam gaps out and lets Gully tell him what to do. Which is to pack everything he owns—clothes, books, laptop, iPod—into Gully's black Tacoma parked in the underground garage. Then they drive to Dunlane.

Gully decides there won't be a funeral service. It's too far for Laverne to travel, and Monica didn't have a lot of other friends, just clients. So who would come? The press and TV crews, and all the curious or just plain nosy townspeople who knew Monica way back when. And that would be a disaster.

Liam agrees, but still, he assumed his mom would have a funeral. That it would be like his grandmother's funeral two years ago, with visiting hours and a minister and hymns. With Gully delivering a eulogy, and then more prayers and readings at the graveside.

Gully also decides that Monica will be buried in Dunlane's Mount Hope & Glory Cemetery. In the Hall family plot beside her mother. Liam knows that's not what she would have wanted. But what can he do? Gully is calling the shots. He won't hear of cremation, and he won't bury his daughter anywhere else.

So Liam and Gully and the cemetery caretaker stand in awkward silence beside a hole in the ground on a sunny May afternoon. That's it. A simple interment. Finally, as they each throw a hunk of dirt on the coffin, Liam whispers, "Be at peace, Mom. Love you always."

Then a couple of cemetery workers lower her into the ground and start shovelling the heap of earth beside her grave on top. The caretaker, some guy called Pete who went to high school with Gully, insists they come look at his office so they don't have to watch.

Pete leads them to what looks like an old stone chapel in the original part of the historic cemetery. He's also president of Friends of Mount Hope & Glory Cemetery and goes on and on about how they restored the building, and all the fascinating records and documents and maps he keeps there. But he sounds so much like a teacher that Liam tunes him out.

Who the hell cares? He should have stayed with his mom while her grave was being filled in. How could he have left her all alone there? And why's this Pete guy looking at him like that? Like Liam's some poor little orphan now. Well, so what? He doesn't want sympathy from people he doesn't even know.

After the boring lecture is over, Gully and Pete decide to go to a bar. Liam hurries back to his mom's grave. The workers have finished and gone. He sits and stares at the baskets of flowers they've arranged on the mound of earth over her. One from Laverne, one from Mr. Cash & Condo, one from Gully's work. And then there's the wreath of pink roses Gully ordered for Liam, with a wide silver ribbon that simply reads: *Mom*.

There's already a gravestone for his grandmother. God, how his mom will hate her final resting place. No hope. No glory. Just an eternal catfight with her own mother down there.

And then Liam bawls like a baby. He and his mom didn't have the usual parent/child relationship, but they loved each other. They were bonded. He already misses her more than he can bear.

He knows the full reality of losing her hasn't hit him yet. It's going to get a whole lot worse. And he's no frigging idea how to cope. What's he ever going to do without her?

"You'll stay on here," Gully says the next morning, flipping the French toast he's making for breakfast. "I'd be happy to have you."

Liam glances around the kitchen to avoid making eye contact. He can't imagine living in this little house with Gully. And definitely not in Dunlane, a town his mom ran away from. "Thanks, but I should be getting back to the city." Although where he'll live, he's no clue. "I mean, I appreciate the offer and all, but ..."

But he's leaned on Gully long enough. If he stays here now, he might never leave. And his mom would never forgive him for that.

"Got anywhere else to go?" Gully serves up Liam's plate and adds more egg-dipped bread to the frying pan. Right. When Gully got in touch with Mr. Cash & Condo, the jerk was scared to death his name would be in the news and his wife and kids would find out everything.

He actually tried to pretend he'd never heard of Liam. He claimed he didn't know Monica had a kid, even though he'd given Liam all those sports tickets. Then he insisted he had no financial responsibility and would take legal action if Liam didn't clear out of his condo ASAP.

Liam had figured Mr. Cash & Condo would look out for him, because his mom had said he was a really nice guy and might someday be Liam's stepdad. Not that Liam had ever asked for a father figure. But she felt he both needed and deserved one.

Now though, apart from his money, Liam has no idea what his mom ever saw in Mr. Cash & Condo. He was glad to hear

Gully telling him what he could bloody well do, and threatening to phone Mr. Cash & Condo's wife if he really wanted to see some heavy legal action.

Gully has already found out there's no life insurance or savings for Liam to inherit. So there's no way he can afford his own place. His mom always spent everything she earned. She joked that Mr. Cash & Condo was her retirement plan.

Some joke.

Maybe he could hitch back to the city, quit school and get a job. But he'd probably end up living on the street. And anyway, he kind of likes learning stuff. His mom had her heart set on him going to university. A good reason to settle down with Mr. Cash & Condo, she said. He could fund her son's higher education.

Another joke. Ha, ha, ha.

"And don't even think about quitting school." Gully sits down at the table, pours some maple syrup onto his French toast. "You know that someday there might be an insurance settlement from the accident, if they ever find the driver, and you'd have some money to do what you want. But the investigation and payout could take years. And until then, you should think of this as your home. I'd like to be your legal guardian."

Liam jumps up for more orange juice. He doesn't want a guardian. He wants his mom back. But it's actually pretty big of Gully to offer, considering that before the accident, they'd met on exactly three occasions.

The first one Liam doesn't even remember. His grandparents came to see him when he was born. According to his mom, Gully tried to convince her to come back home to Dunlane and live with them. But Liam's grandmother said if that happened she'd move out. No way was she having her hussy daughter and her out-of-wedlock brat under her roof. Even if they were family.

Then the year Liam was seven, his mom decided they could try going to her parents' place for Christmas. She said it was only fair for him to get to know his grandparents. But that didn't work out either.

His mom and grandmother yelled at each other the whole time. They relived every single issue they'd ever disagreed on—basically everything on earth. Liam and his mom left in the middle of Christmas dinner and caught a bus home.

The third time Liam remembers all too well. He and his mom took the train to Dunlane for his grandmother's funeral. But his mom stayed in their motel room and watched TV while Liam went to the service.

Gully was pretty upset by that. Liam remembers him coming by the motel and begging her to come back to Dunlane, now that her mother was gone. But she still wouldn't.

It's not because of him, she told Liam. I love my dad and I miss him. It's the stupid town of Dunlane. I hate that place. It's a dead end. There's no future for us there.

And now here Liam is. In Dunlane. Gully wants him to stay. Wants to look after him. What's not to like?

Going to school in Dunlane, that's what. If only he could go back to his old school in the city. He didn't have any friends, but he knew the teachers and the way things worked. He got along okay. He doesn't want to deal with a new school.

But mostly he doesn't want to go back to school right away. He can't face explaining to new teachers and kids why he's living here in Dunlane with his grandfather. He needs some time to get over what's happened, pull himself together.

"How about I wait and start back in the fall?" he says to Gully as he clears his plate. "Great breakfast by the way. Thanks."

Gully says, "There's six weeks left in the academic year. You can take the rest of this one off, but you're living with me, and you're going to school."

Mistakes

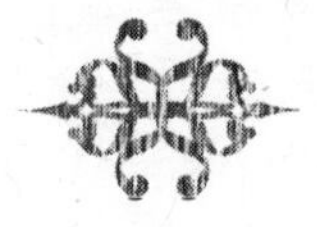

Hey Rue,

I'm writing to you because Sarita says that if I don't want to go to the support group for grieving teens she runs, then keeping a journal of my feelings might help me deal with things. She says I have the right to mourn you in a way that works for me, to express my feelings in my own way, but lots of people find a journal is the answer.

Huh? Does she really believe it will be helpful for me to obsess about what happened? Because if I have to remember and think about everything to write it down, I'll keep you alive in my mind and heart forever. Instead of letting you go, which is what everybody says I'm supposed to do. What I need to do so I can move on.

Sarita says that unresolved grief can hurt you forever. And honestly, she'll never give up hoping that someday I'll be ready to join her group, which is mostly for kids who've lost a parent or sibling, but she says I could still benefit. I told her I've absolutely zero interest in meeting other kids mourning a death. So then she got really creative and suggested I start a blog. That way, I could talk about my feelings anonymously online and maybe get some helpful comments, and at least realize I'm not alone. And that would help me begin healing.

Blogging about my broken heart is so not me. Like I want to share my sorrow with the whole world. I don't get the appeal of going public with the details of my pathetic life so far. But then, maybe that's because of all the dirty nasty *lies* Christine posted about me on Facebook. Or maybe it's because of that video she posted on YouTube featuring me doing something embarrassing and shameful with a certain guy at a certain party. When that went viral, well, I started wanting to keep some things just a bit more private.

But I promised Sarita I'd at least try, so I've found this notebook to write in. I want to keep my word, because despite what I've just said about her I have to admit that Sarita has already helped me a lot. A whole lot. She defended me in the hospital when I was weak and confused and overwhelmed. I owe her.

So maybe I'll just start by telling you a bit about me, since we never really got to know each other very well. My name is Harmony Trahern and I'm almost sixteen. I'm an only child and my parents were really ancient when they had me, so they act more like they're my grandparents, and yes, they actually would have been your grandparents. We live in Dunlane, Ontario, this really hopeless town that has seen better days. Mom claims it was a real happening place back in the nineteenth century though.

Anyway, our house was built in 1871 by Doran McRory, a cabinetmaker, which explains the amazing woodwork inside. The outside is painted white with green shutters, roof and door, and there's one of those blue historic plaques in our front yard. Tourists often stop and take photos of McRory House, because it's listed on a walking tour of Dunlane as being of historical significance.

McRory House is the only place I've ever lived. Every once in a while my parents talk about moving to a condo in Kingston, but I doubt they ever will. Not even if I were to fulfill their dearest hopes and go to law school at Queen's so I can work for Legal Aid or Lawyers Without Borders and change the world. We have never moved. Apparently my parents spent so many carefree years travelling around the world before I was born that when they finally settled down here in Dunlane—because they could buy their dream historic house for next to nothing—they were completely content. I'd like to tell you that they lived happily ever after, but of course they didn't, because of what happened, which we'll get to later. Or another time. Anyway, I'm not sure what my parents will do when I someday leave home. I don't think they're prepared for the empty nest thing at all. I guess that's why they were so supportive of me having you, and wanted to help me raise you.

You should know, if you haven't already figured it out, that my parents are a bit weird. They aren't like other people. Or at least, not like the good people of Dunlane. Not even like the bad ones either. I don't mean that they're aliens or anything—my parents, not Dunlaners—although they could all certainly qualify. The story my parents tell is that they were flower-power teenagers in the psychedelic sixties (yes Rue, so embarrassing), then dropped out of university to protest wars, hitch around Europe, sleep on beaches in Greece and Morocco, and search for enlightenment in India. They're still hippies at heart. And true to their hippie nature, they like to go barefoot, eat soy products that do not harm animals, and sometimes smoke pot to feel groovy. Oh, and they don't like big business or the government, but they do believe in free love and the mystical power of the universe. And if that sounds like a hippie stereotype to you, well, you just might be onto something.

You should also know that some people say my parents, Nolan and Daisy (or Noodle and Dazey, as I've thought of them since I was ten, but don't worry, nobody else knows that, and I would never call them that in public), are John and Yoko look-alikes. Of course you're way too young to have heard of John Lennon and Yoko Ono, but they were a long-ago power couple famous for singing and promoting world peace and sex by lying in hotel beds for days, or something like that. My parents are so thrilled and proud when anybody mentions their resemblance to these role models. It makes them feel all young-at-heart and connected, which is hard to understand because as I said, it all happened ages ago. They've even suggested that instead of Noodle and Dazey I might like to call them John and Yoko, which I just can't do. The whole thing makes me feel like hiding from my parents in a strawberry field, or escaping in a yellow submarine.

My dad grew up in England when the Beatles were just becoming famous. The Beatles is the name of the band that John Lennon sang with. Dad has every record the Beatles ever made and he wears his brown hair long and parted in the middle, just like John used to. This is to perpetuate the look-alike thing. When Dad wants to imagine that he's the reincarnation of John Lennon (who was assassinated!), say on a warm summer evening, he puts on his round wire-rimmed glasses (totally fake, btw, he wears contacts) and gets out his guitar. Then he sits on the verandah strumming chords. I have never heard Noodle actually sing an entire Beatles song start to finish. He simply can't remember all the words. I sometimes wonder if he has severe memory loss from his youthful years of travelling and tripping. Or from his continued use of what he now calls the wonderful wacky weed. But he says what's important isn't so much the exact lyrics, but the mind-blowing feelings.

My mom, whose ancestors are Welsh, French, Russian and Asian, but who grew up in boring old Canada, has long, straight hair dyed jet black (again with the look-alike thing), dark eyes and great legs. Because my parents lived in England for years, Mom can talk with a very convincing British accent if she wants to impress someone. Which she hardly ever does. She is so above what anybody thinks of her. Unless they're saying she looks like Yoko. (Dad never uses his accent, unless he's singing a line from a Beatles song.) But I suspect Mom talks like the Queen during parent/teacher interviews, and for sure I heard her doing it when she was arguing with the hospital staff.

Anyway, out back of our house there's an old stable that Dad converted into a shop. There he sells the furniture he refinishes and the antiques he buys at auction. He calls his place The Barley Sugar Barn. He says barley sugar is a kind of candy he loved as a kid, and he keeps a jar of it—an old-fashioned penny candy jar of course—on the counter. It is yummy, I can tell you that, and apparently customers love barley sugar too, because Dad's always having to buy more. Dazey calls The Barley Sugar Barn the B.S. Barn and thinks that's the funniest joke ever. When The Barley Sugar Barn is open—all summer and then weekends for the rest of the year—people come and buy chairs and tables and quaint old collectibles like oil lamps and cheese dishes and brass candlesticks.

Mom also sells pre-owned stuff, but she prefers the 24/7 hours of eBay. She mostly deals in old books and prints and vintage clothes. Me, I've never had a job, except going to auctions and flea markets and garage sales with my parents and helping choose what to buy and then helping load it into our van to truck home. I've never even babysat or anything (Which must make you wonder what your level of personal care would have been if you'd stuck around, but I would have figured it out in time, I promise). When I'm not busy working as an antiques consultant, or doing the physical labour that involves, I mostly like to read fantasy novels. They inspire me to dress up in cool costumes to escape my sad little life.

I also like to shop, just not at the Dunlane Mall anymore. Now I only buy clothes at thrift stores or garage sales or on eBay. I don't have any friends left, except you, Rue, and I'm not sure if you count. A lot of people, including the doctors and nurses, said that you don't. And even if you do, I guess you would be a relative, not exactly a friend. And I have to tell you that there are days when I'm scared you were only ever just a figment of my very sick imagination. But no. I never could get the bloodstains out of my jeans. You were real. You *are* real.

So yeah, most kids avoid me. Some ignore me because I'm not in this loser gang called Y4C, which stands for Youth 4 Crime, if you can believe anybody giving a gang a stupid name like that. And some won't speak to me because I almost did join. I went to this outrageous party at the cemetery last Halloween (when that video I mentioned that ended up on YouTube was shot) and word got around. I know, I know, I'm totally embarrassed and ashamed, but I was a lot younger last fall. I was trusting and innocent and didn't have a clue.

It's so important to me that you know I wasn't always a freak. Please believe me: *I used to be normal*. I was best friends with Christine Dobrinski and guys called me all the time. But I never liked any of them for more than two weeks. They called me the Ice Queen Supreme and that was fine by me. I'd fool around a bit, but nothing more. My parents encouraged me to experiment with sex but to keep my options open and not get tied down to a steady boyfriend. They were always on about no one owning another person and of course the importance of birth control. But they didn't need to worry, because I knew what I was doing. Or so I thought. My rule was that I was in control, not the guy.

And everything was fine until Jordan Yale showed up at Dunlane District High School. I remembered him from elementary school. I hadn't seen him for years, because he'd been away at boarding schools since grade nine. But he'd been kicked out of all of them, and now his parents didn't know what else to do. So they gave up and sent him to DDHS. Who knows, maybe they thought that would teach him an important life lesson, seeing how the masses live. But probably it was just the worst possible punishment they could think of.

There were a lot of wild rumours about Jordan, but that didn't matter to me. It just made him more attractive. He'd gone from being a geeky ten-year-old to the coolest guy on earth. You know that old saying about how the bigger they are, the harder they fall? Well, the Ice Queen Supreme fell. Hard. And after I fell, I melted into a little puddle of brainless love at Jordan Yale's feet. *I would have done anything to be his girlfriend.*

When Jordan talked about forming a gang to give kids power it seemed like an awesome idea. Genius! After all, I'd grown up hearing my parents talk about revolution and changing the world. I know it seems incredibly naive now, but I really thought that Jordan wanted to start something cool like Save the Children. I was so blinded by love I didn't get that he'd turned into a messed up, insecure bully who just wanted attention. I didn't know he was going to call his pathetic gang Youth 4 Crime. And for sure I didn't know the terrible things they were going to do.

So okay, I made some mistakes. Please, please, please don't think I mean you, Rue. I'm not saying that you personally were a mistake. But okay, to be completely honest,

I have to contradict myself and tell you that you kind of were. So is that why you decided to turn back? Because you thought I didn't want you? Ohmigod, I hope not. I did my best, you know? I tried so hard to accept you. And by the time you left I really, really wanted you and now I am so, so sorry. You are gone and I have empty arms and a broken, aching heart.

Oh great, now I'm getting all weepy and upset and feeling like I'm having another breakdown. Maybe it's one of those "griefbursts" Sarita warned me about. I knew this writing about stuff was going to be crap. I'd like to call Sarita and ask her how exactly this is supposed to be helping me? Because I feel about a million times worse than I did a few minutes ago.

Threats

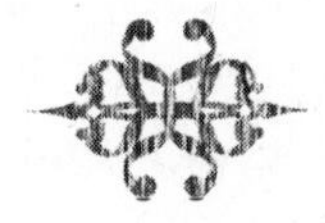

After the May holiday weekend, Liam starts at Dunlane District High School with dread. He's looked at the DDHS website and learned how different it's going to be. His old school had only about 600 kids. More than half of them were new immigrants and/or ESL students. The focus was academic and almost everybody wanted to go to university. There are 1200 students at DDHS, mostly white, who've always lived in Dunlane or are bussed in from rural areas. The dropout rate is high.

His mom went to DDHS. Look how good she turned out. He knows that's bitter. But he can't help feeling mixed up about her. Especially after seeing the headline in the local newspaper over the weekend: "Hometown Queen Dies Tragically." The story says that his mom was Miss Dunlane 1996. Something she neglected to share with her son. He'd had no idea.

And it makes him wonder what else she didn't tell him.

When she was alive he could pretend he didn't care what his mom did to earn money. He was able to block it out. But now she's dead he's suddenly so pissed at her. What was she thinking, selling herself? Didn't she care what kind of example she was setting? Didn't she wonder how her son would feel? Didn't she know it would keep him from ever being normal?

How's he supposed to go to DDHS? Kids will want to hear all the gory details of his mom's accident. If one of them guesses the truth, he couldn't handle it.

He feels like hurling as he walks through the doors. But as the day wears on, it looks like he needn't have worried. Nobody gives a rat's ass.

Except for his English teacher, who says she remembers his mom. She actually taught Monica when Monica was in high school. How big a coincidence is that?

Ms. Smythe gushes on about how sorry she is and all. But her face says something else. Something like: *So your mom was failing English because even though she was smart she couldn't be bothered with school and then she went and got pregnant and she always was a bit of a slut, that Monica Hall.*

And then after school this guy with his arms covered in tattoos comes up to Liam's locker. He's wearing a grungy T-shirt, filthy camouflage pants and boots with big silver buckles. "Hey Ghoul Guy," he says. "Saw ya in the graveyard." He's kind of scary, but also kind of cool. He stands and speaks like somebody who makes kids want to do what he says.

"So?" Liam's been to his mom's grave every day since she was buried. He takes her flowers from Gully's garden. He sits with her and thinks about things. "It's a public place."

The guy flexes his left arm so one particular tattoo pops up on his biceps: *Y4C4EVR!* With his right arm he pushes Liam up against his locker. "It's *my* place. The cemetery belongs to me and Y4C."

Y4C? Sounds like a postal code. But Liam knows better than to actually say that. Or mock the guy's stupid tattoo. The pressure on his chest is making it hard to breath though, so he pushes back. "You and *who?*"

The guy doesn't answer. He tries to force Liam into his locker again. "Heard your old lady kicked it."

"It was a hit-and-run." Liam pushes back, hard enough to make the guy take his hands off. "Got that, a-hole?"

"I also heard that Mama's little boy likes to cry on her grave."

Liam is tempted to yank out the guy's nose ring. Or one of his ear studs. But he resists. Don't lower yourself with violence, his mom would say. It's never a solution. There's always another choice. He looks at the guy and shrugs. "So? Big frigging deal."

The guy gets right in his face then, giving Liam a good look at his teeth. They're straight and shiny and scream spoiled-rich-kid-playing-badass. "So you either hang with us," the guy snarls, "or you stay away from the cemetery."

Liam looks up and down the hall. "And who would us be, exactly?"

The guy jerks his head toward the girl working a biker-chick look who's been standing nearby talking on a cellphone. She pockets her phone and comes over to pat his butt. "Hey babe," she says.

"This is Crime," he says. "I'm Youth."

Liam stifles a laugh. *Crime*? *Youth*? He wouldn't dare make fun of their gang names, but please. Those are so wuss. No street cred at all.

"We got a lot of friends," Youth says. "They're all just called 4."

"4?" And here Liam was thinking this guy and his gang couldn't get any wimpier.

"That would be as in Youth 4 Crime," Crime says. "Y4C. We party in the cemetery. You can be a 4, but you gotta do what we say."

Y4C? What kind of gang name is that? And, you gotta do what we say? What is this guy? Like ten years old or something? Liam stares down at his high tops, as if he's actually afraid.

Bad move. It makes him remember how his mom bought him those sneakers only two weeks ago. They cost a lot, but she wanted him to have the latest clothes and stuff. Now she'll never know what he's wearing. Or what he's doing.

She'll never say, hey, your hair looks good, or, how'd your test go today?

She'll never stock the freezer with his favourite pizza and ice cream again.

She'll never make roasted veggie lasagna for dinner and try to convince him it's better than anything made with meat, that he really should go vegetarian.

And all of a sudden he's afraid he's going to lose it. He's going to break down and cry right in front of Youth and Crime. Because when he's not mad at his mom, he misses her so much.

"You hear me?" Youth says. "You wanna be a 4, you belong to us."

"Nice. And if I don't?"

Youth hugs Crime. "Then the whole school's gonna know what a crybaby you are."

"Wow, I'm scared." Youth and Crime are such posers. Liam's old school was way tougher. It was full of high achievers, but there were kids he was really afraid of. Kids he'd go out of his way to avoid. Kids he knew had ties to serious gangs that wouldn't mind knifing you in the parking lot. Or worse.

"We don't like crybabies," Youth says. "And we don't wanna see you in the graveyard again unless you're a 4."

"Dude." Liam straightens up and squares his shoulders, a move he's learned from Gully. "I'll do whatever I want."

Youth shrugs and shakes his head. "You been warned, Ghoul Guy."

As they leave, Crime turns back and gives Liam a flirty smile. She's kind of hot, even with all that black eyeliner. She sticks out her pierced tongue and licks slowly at her chin and then all along her upper lip. "Remember," she says, taking out her cell-phone. "We'll be watching ya."

That night at dinner Gully asks, "So how was school?"

"Okay." Yeah, right. One of his teachers remembers his mom, and not in a good way. He's already had words with Y4C's leader Youth and his girlfriend Crime. He's already known as Ghoul Guy. "I can probably get all my credits."

Gully is dressed in his work uniform. Light blue shirt over a black T-shirt. Both tucked into navy cargo pants. Polished black boots with steel toes. Liam's not sure why, since Gully's shift doesn't start until eleven. But he has a feeling this is for his sake—like Gully thinks he's showing him who's boss or presenting a strong parental image or something. Because he says, "Your mom made some bad choices, Liam."

"I guess." Does Gully really think he needs reminding?

Gully pokes at his spaghetti. He made the sauce himself, with tomatoes he had in the freezer from his garden last summer. "And I really hope you won't do the same."

What, like have a kid on his own before he finishes high school? Become a—well, never mind. "Not likely." But then again, Youth, Crime and Y4C are after him. Who knows what he might have to do to survive in Dunlane. Even though he's not scared of them, he knows they're not going to leave him be. They're going to give him trouble. Major trouble. "I mean, I'll try not to."

"You're a smart kid, but this is a tough town. You don't want a criminal record." Gully's a guard—a corrections officer—at Millhaven. It's a maximum-security prison between Dunlane and Kingston, packed with hundreds of the country's most dangerous criminals. "And you sure as hell don't want to go to prison."

"I know that." Liam's seen enough movies with scenes set in prisons. He'd be terrified of being raped or murdered or forced to fight in a riot. Maybe someday he can get Gully to tell him what it's really like inside. He probably has some cool stories.

"Thing is—" Gully's voice catches. Liam knows he's hurting. Gully tried so hard to reach out to his daughter, but she rejected him every time. And now she's dead. And they can barely mention her. It's just too hard to admit she's gone, or talk about how she got killed or how she earned her money.

So far all Gully's said is stuff like he wishes he'd called her more often. He wishes he'd tried even harder to get Monica's mother to forgive her. But on the other hand he's glad her mother isn't alive to suffer through this, because having her daughter die in a hit-and-run would have killed her.

Liam wipes the last of his grandfather's delicious tomato sauce off his plate with a hunk of crusty garlic bread. So this is where his mom learned to cook. The sauce tastes just like something she would have made. No meat, lots of herbs and spices and veggies.

"What I want to say is," Gully tries again, "there's kids here in Dunlane totally out of control." He twirls some spaghetti around his fork and points it at Liam. "Stay away from them."

Swarm

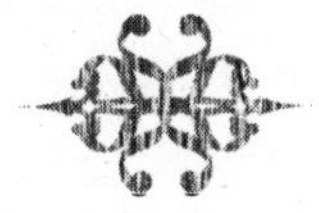

There's nothing much to do in Dunlane. Not that Liam feels like doing anything. But sometimes he really needs to get out of Gully's little house. It's about the size of a camper van. Not nearly as big as Mr. Cash & Condo's condo. But at least it's not the house his mom grew up in. That would be too weird.

Gully says he moved after Liam's grandmother died, because he wanted less house to look after, more garden to work, and no sad memories. From the street this place looks like a dollhouse sitting in a huge park. And there are no mementos inside. Nothing to suggest Gully ever had a wife or a daughter. Except for one photo in a silver frame in his office, now Liam's bedroom.

It's the photo the newspaper used in the article about Monica's death, showing her as Miss Dunlane 1996. So Liam guesses this means that her being hometown queen is a happy memory for Gully. She's riding in a red Mustang convertible, wearing a cheesy crown and a strapless white dress. She's laughing and holding a big bouquet of long-stemmed red and white roses.

Was she already pregnant when that picture was taken? And why didn't she ever tell Liam about being Miss Dunlane? Man, that hurts.

Gully also showed Liam the original article, neatly clipped and folded away in his desk drawer. The desk where Liam now does his homework. The article said that Monica was picked to be Miss Dunlane out of ten contestants and crowned at the Canada Day celebrations.

She won by giving an inspiring speech about recycling and then performing a dynamite song and dance medley from *Fame* for the selection committee and a crowd of over two hundred. She was supposed to represent the town of Dunlane at public functions all the next year.

But she didn't. Seventeen-year-old Miss Dunlane 1996 smiled and wore her crown and carried her flowers in the parade, then disappeared.

The story of his mom's glory days makes Liam feel like running into the street and throwing himself in front of a truck. He wants to die, too. His mom was all he had. And now she's gone. Plus he's stuck with the idea that he didn't really know her at all.

She had secrets. Things she never told him. And when he starts thinking like that, he has to escape. He has to go somewhere, do something, to keep from freaking out.

But Main Street, the only place besides school and the cemetery that he can walk to, looks like a movie set from the 1950s. It's a few blocks of useless stores and if there's anybody around they're wrinklies who've lived in Dunlane forever.

If this were the city there'd be trendy shops and funky cafes. But it's not. It's Dunlane, and all the good stuff—the cinema complex, mall and fast food strip—are way out by the 401 Highway. Too far to walk and there's no bus.

Gully says he'll drive Liam wherever he wants to go, but then he'd have to come pick him up too. Liam doesn't want to be any more dependent on him than he already is. He misses living where he could hop on a streetcar or subway and go wherever he liked. Back in his old life, he spent most of his free time exploring the city.

That and swimming lengths in the pool at Mr. Cash & Condo's condo. But there's no pool here in Dunlane. Lake Ontario is nearby, with miles of great parks and beaches and sand dunes. But of course he'd need a ride to get there.

He's also heard that just north of town there's a giant, leaking landfill site. But he wouldn't go there even if he did have his licence and a car. No wonder Dunlane is also known as DumpLane.

No wonder his mom didn't want to live here. Liam doesn't want to either. But right now he doesn't have much choice.

So he goes to school, watches TV, plays video games and wanders the streets. Some kids would turn to drinking or drugs, but he's not into that. His mom would kill him. Well, if she wasn't already dead herself, and she wasn't against violence of any kind. Substance abuse is not an acceptable way of dealing with stress, she'd say. As far as she was concerned, it was right up there with eating meat.

He longs to go to the cemetery to visit his mom. It's so painful not to. But he has the feeling it might be even more painful, in a different way, if he did. Because he really doesn't want to join Youth 4 Crime.

They're not even a real gang; just a bunch of bored kids who think it's cool to be bad. So he has to play it safe for a while. He has to wait until they don't care about him anymore. Until they find somebody else to harass.

Not that he's seen Youth or Crime around school. Maybe they're in co-op. Maybe they go to the offsite program for kids who don't do well in a regular classroom. Maybe they're acting invisible on purpose to psych him out. Or maybe they just skip. He doesn't know. But what he does know is that they haven't forgotten him.

He knows because of what he finds stuffed in his homeroom desk. It's a page ripped out of a notebook with a crude drawing of a gravestone with a big black X scrawled over it. Then there's something red that looks like drops of blood or maybe tears splattered all around. And the next day he finds graffiti all over his locker. *Ghoul Guy! Y4C! Y4C4EVR!*

What can he do but keep his head down? Pretend not to notice. Act like he couldn't care less. And keep away from the cemetery.

Then Gully asks him to run an errand. He needs Liam to pick up some garden twine at the hardware store down on Main Street on his way home from school. Liam doesn't mind at all. He's grateful for something different to do. It'll take a few minutes off the lonely empty hours that await him when he does get home. And it's also the least he can do for Gully.

He's just going into the store when he sees a gang of kids across the street. There's maybe fifteen of them coming out of the pizza place, stuffing their faces with huge greasy slices. He has a sinking feeling they all belong to Youth 4 Crime.

And then he sees that Youth and Crime are there with them, kind of herding them from behind. Youth is yelling f-this! and f-that! Crime is dancing around, shimmying and writhing, getting everybody all worked up.

A couple more kids come along with dogs on leashes, big scary dogs that are growling and barking like mad.

"Hey Ghoul Guy!" Youth shouts across the street. "Get your ass over here."

He's doomed. It's quiet in downtown Dunlane. Not many shoppers about, not much traffic. No help in sight.

Crime shakes her fists in the air and screams, "We're gonna have some fun!"

Just then a little old lady comes out of the bank and starts shuffling along the sidewalk. It's a warm day but she's wearing a long coat and a wooly hat like it's the middle of winter. In one hand she's carrying a purse and a cloth shopping bag with a loaf of bread sticking out. In the other hand she holds a cane.

She's walking slowly and carefully in her sensible shoes, watching the sidewalk like she's afraid she'll trip and fall, using her cane to guide her. She doesn't even see them coming.

But suddenly there's whooping and hooting and they're swarming her. They're shrieking with laughter as they knock her down. She tries to fight them off with her cane until someone kicks it out of her hand. The cane goes flying and the old lady gives a shocked cry that turns into a hopeless scream.

Liam can't make himself respond. He just stands there as they punch her and kick her and grab her bag and her purse. Then she stops struggling. Her cries fade into pained moaning as they strip off her jewellery. They even stomp on her loaf of bread. Then they throw it to the dogs, who sink their teeth into it and try to rip it away from each other.

He knows he should go help her. But he still doesn't. Don't get involved, that's what his mom taught him about witnessing stuff on the street. Mind your own business. Stay clear and save yourself.

But this is brutal!

Now one of girls picks up the cane and starts hitting the old lady over the head and back with it. It makes a sickening sound, whack, whack, whack. The dogs drop the bread and begin another barking frenzy.

And then as suddenly as it started, it's over. With a lot of swearing and yelling *Y4C4EVR!* they're gone. They take off in all directions down the side streets, leaving the poor old lady lying there on the sidewalk. A couple of cars go by, but the drivers don't seem to notice her. She's not moving and she's not making a sound. Liam can still hear those stupid dogs barking in the distance.

What happens next he's totally ashamed of. Because instead of doing the right thing, instead of running over to see if she's okay, he acts like a coward. He pretends nothing happened and hurries on into the hardware store. Because even though they're gone, Youth and Crime know that he saw what Y4C did. And that binds him to them in a way he doesn't want.

Helping that old lady and giving a statement to the cops would only make things worse. He'd get a beating too. And although he noticed that Youth and Crime didn't do any of the dirty work themselves—just egged the others on—something tells him they'd want the fun of punishing him.

He does watch through the store window to make sure that somebody helps the old lady. He can see folks rushing out of other stores and gathering around. Someone with a cellphone is making a call. By the time Liam has found and paid for Gully's garden twine an ambulance is already on the scene. As he leaves the store, paramedics are examining the old lady, giving her oxygen and lifting her onto a stretcher.

When he gets home, Gully thanks him for stopping by the hardware store like Liam's done the nicest thing. Which makes him feel like shit. If Gully only knew what Liam didn't do for that old lady.

The incident is written up in the local paper. Gully brings it in from the front porch when he comes home from work the next morning. Liam is sitting at the kitchen table eating some toast when Gully slams the paper down and says, "Unbelievable!" Liam stares at the front page, trying to think fast what to say about it.

Gully points to the colour photo of the old lady lying in a hospital bed with her arm in a cast, hooked up to all kinds of monitors and tubes. "Know anything about this?" His voice carries thirty years of prison guard experience. "Seems to me you were down on Main Street about that time yesterday."

Liam reads the headline: "Swarming on Main Street: Youth Crime on the Rise in Dunlane." He glances at the article.

Yesterday afternoon a senseless attack by a local youth gang left a helpless senior in serious condition in hospital. They stole her money, her jewellery and her dignity. They left her with a broken wrist, severe bruising, and a concussion. Dunlane OPP detachment expressed frustration with their limited resources to fight the growing problem of youth crime in our town. Several incidents of random violence and vandalism over the past year have left citizens living in fear.

"That's terrible!" Liam says. "But no, I didn't see anything."

"You sure about that?"

"Yeah, it must have happened after I left Main Street." And he does sound sure, probably because he spent all night trying to convince himself he wasn't a witness.

Living in the city he saw a lot of stuff go down on the street. Seriously bad stuff. But never anything so senseless and cold-blooded—kids beating and robbing a helpless old lady! She didn't provoke them, and she didn't look like she owed them money or anything. They had absolutely no reason to attack her. No reason except getting off on violence.

It makes him want to puke.

"Who would do something like that?" Gully says.

"Total jerks." A.k.a. Youth and Crime and Y4C. "Honest, I don't know anything about it."

He hopes Gully believes him. He's acting so cool he almost believes himself. But he doesn't know Gully well enough yet to tell if he's fooled him with his lies or not. He opens his math textbook and says, "Gotta finish this homework. But if I hear anything around school, I'll pass it on."

Gully pours himself some coffee. "Problem is, every kid in Dunlane knows they can get away with murder because there's not enough cops in this place."

"Um, yeah, kids do talk about that at school." The word is that there are only two OPP officers in town. They serve a huge rural area as well as the town itself. And they're always busy with car crashes and speeders up on the highway. Or busting grow-ops out in the country. "Most kids think the cops are a total joke."

At least that's what he's overheard. It's not like anybody actually speaks to him at school. Except for teachers, especially his mom's old English teacher, Ms. Smythe.

She seems to be making an effort to help Liam fit in. Maybe she feels guilty she didn't stop his mom from ruining her life or something. But teachers don't count.

Still, he's starting to feel accepted because kids who are 4s don't stop talking when he's around. They don't act like they think he'll rat them out. Mostly they don't seem to know what to make of him.

City kid. Dead mom. Ghoul Guy.

They don't have a lot in common.

Unless Liam becomes a 4. Which is so not going to happen.

Gully grunts and stretches, peels off his work shirt. "Putting the garden in on Sunday," he says, unlacing his boots. "Tomato time. I could use your help."

What a relief. They're off the topic of the swarming. "Sure," Liam says. Why not help Gully when he's done so much for him? And it's probably wise to stay on Gully's good side. And okay, it's not like Liam's got anything else to do. "Sure, I'd be glad to help." Over the past couple weeks Gully's been getting the soil in his huge garden ready for planting. He's rototilled it and added heaps of compost and raked it all smooth. "Mom told me a lot about your garden. Well, the one you had when she was growing up."

Gully stops in the middle of taking off his boots. He stands awkwardly on one foot and tilts his head as if he thinks Liam's making this up but can't figure out why. "She did?"

"Yeah, she did." Liam's surprised to find he wants to give Gully something happy here. "There was lots of stuff she wouldn't talk about, but she said that her best childhood memories were of helping you in your garden."

But Gully looks like he's going to start howling with grief, so Liam doesn't add that she also told him how she used to have her own vegetable patch and how much she liked looking after it. How that was the beginning of her wanting to be a vegetarian. And how she was planning to buy some planters for herbs and tomatoes for their balcony on the 24th of May weekend. Mr. Cash & Condo's place was the first time they'd ever lived anywhere she could garden.

But she never got to do that. She got run down and killed instead. "So, crack of dawn Sunday morning?" Liam says.

Gully finishes taking off his boots. "Oh, I'll let you sleep in until eight, how's that?"

"Cool."

"And stay out of trouble until then, okay?"

"No problem."

Harm

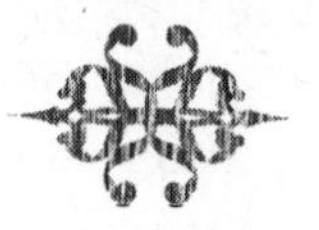

Hey Rue,

Maybe it's a good thing you didn't enter the world as we know it. I'm almost sure you're somewhere much safer and happier. Somewhere heavenly. I picture fluffy clouds and shimmering light all around your tiny pure soul, lifting you up above the world of human horrors. Horrors like what happened on Main Street the other day. I so hope you didn't see that. Y4C swarmed a helpless old lady! They robbed her and beat her so badly she had to be hospitalized. Why would they do that? What were they thinking? Oh right, they weren't thinking. They're just a bunch of brain-dead kids acting out their most savage instincts.

I hate Youth and his evil gang. I can't believe I was ever involved with such a loser, even if it was before he gave himself that ridiculous name. How could I ever have been seriously crushing on Jordan Yale? Yeah sure, he used to be good at school and sports before he started amusing himself and annoying his parents by playing at being a young offender. And he used to be handsome, before he started trying to be edgy by dressing like a punk and getting all those tattoos. But why did he have so much power over me? And it's not just me. Lots of other kids fell under his spell too.

I guess it's partly because he acts so confident, like he's entitled to have and do whatever he wants. He doesn't live by the rules—he makes them. And he found the one way to attract my attention. He played hard to get. I don't like that guys throw themselves at me because they think I'm pretty in a fashion magazine kind of way, but I'm used to it. And okay, it's flattering. So when Jordan didn't hit on me, when he seemed to look right past me, I wondered why. And the more he ignored me, the more I tried to get him to notice me. How shallow is that? I only wanted him because he wasn't interested.

At least that's how it started. Then I really fell for him. I'd gone out with lots of guys, but never with any one of them for long, so I didn't have that much experience in how these things worked. It's hard to believe now, but I really had no idea Jordan was manipulating me. I really thought we were meant to be together. You'd think *someone* would have told me, but apparently *she* had other plans.

So you're probably wondering what happened.

Well, I know it sounds childish, but I got caught up in this idea Jordan had to hold a party in the cemetery on Halloween night. I thought everybody would dress in magical costumes and there'd be candles and those outdoor torches and carved jack-o-lanterns. I was that innocent. I wore this purple velvet, medieval princess dress and made up a story for my parents about a Halloween party at Christine Dobrinski's house. Since she was still my best friend back then, and since I'd known her since kindergarten, they had no reason not to believe me. Dad even gave me a ride to Christine's place. Not that I had to hide where I was really going from Noodle and Dazey—they probably would have been cool with the cemetery party thing. But Jordan had made this big deal about everybody keeping it all top secret. And so did Christine, like half the fun was going to be fooling our parents.

When Dad dropped me off I was kind of surprised to see that Christine was just wearing jeans and a tight, black top and a lot of goth makeup. We'd been texting all week about what we were going to wear and had decided that I'd go as a fantasy princess and she'd go as a mythical bird. We both already had the costumes. Mom had made mine because I loved dressing up like characters from my favourite novels and Christine was going to borrow hers from her sister, who'd worn it in a ballet recital. When I asked Christine what was up with that, why she wasn't wearing her costume, she said that her sister needed it for another party. Then she said she wasn't really all that into the costume thing anyway. So we gave out candy to the little trick-or-treaters who came by her house and then we walked to the cemetery.

And when we got there I saw why Christine wasn't dressed up as a feathery bird. Nobody else was wearing an actual costume but me. Some kids had wigs or witch hats, temporary tattoos or fake wounds, but I was the only purple velvet princess. I was so pissed off. Why didn't you tell me? I asked Christine. She just made a face like her mascara was flaking into her eyes. I realized that she'd been acting a bit strange for the last while, like she didn't want to be best friends anymore but didn't know how to tell me. Was this how she was dumping me? Setting me up to look like a dork at Jordan's cemetery party?

Yes. It was. Because she wanted him for herself. I found out later that she'd been after Jordan all along. She'd planned the whole costume thing so she could make me look like a loser. She took pictures with her cellphone and posted them on Facebook. And as I might have mentioned before, she even recorded certain other events for YouTube.

All so that I'd seem undesirable and Jordan would go for her instead of me. Talk about manipulation.

But back to the party. Okay, so I had a few drinks. Jordan had a camping cooler and he dumped all the booze anybody brought into it. He called it Devil's Blood Punch and it tasted like the cheap red wine it mostly was, but I was trying to save face and pay Christine back for the costume thing so I choked it down. I'm not really sure what else happened or how or when things got out of control. I remember being giggly and then dizzy and then Jordan saying it was time to test me. I had to prove I was wild enough to be his girlfriend.

He said he'd always wanted to fool around on a grave with a virgin. Of course I said no to that, but I was mad at Christine, and, okay, I was kind of drunk. So I helped him break into the caretaker's office, and while we were in there doing whatever we did, which is the part I can't or don't want to remember, everybody else went crazy. Kids started raging around, setting grass fires and knocking over gravestones, and when Jordan and I came out of the office we joined in. But that could all be lies. Courtesy of Christine. Who posted a message on my Facebook wall about how slutty and shameless I'd been, and how she never wanted to hang out with me again. I don't really trust what she said I'd done, but I don't trust my own memory either. I couldn't face looking at the photos or the video she posted. I took my profile down and I've never looked at Facebook or YouTube again..

If only I could remember what I did. And not just the vandalism. The sex. There, I've said it. I admit to having sex with Youth, although at least it was back when he was still called Jordan. But that's not the worst thing. What I really hate is that I have no idea what my first time was like. Except that I know for sure it wasn't romantic. And we definitely weren't in love. It's all a blur that still makes me want to vomit, and I regret it so much, but I can't change what happened.

There was a big fuss in town about the party in the cemetery and the damage we did. Kids who'd been there started calling it the Legend of the Lost Tombstones. I felt so terrible that I might have violated somebody's grave. I felt betrayed and humiliated by Christine and lost without my best friend. And I also had the added worry that I might have had unprotected sex with Youth. Based on the physical evidence I washed off my body the next day, I was pretty sure we hadn't used a condom. The trouble was, I could never ask him because there was always a bunch of kids hanging around him. He was never alone. I didn't want to phone or text him about it. I had to see him face to face.

Finally one day I saw him sitting in the school cafeteria and I waited until everybody else left and I sat down beside him and kind of whispered my question into his ear. He burst out laughing. Don't go all weird on me, he said. Then he told me the name he'd picked for his gang: Youth 4 Crime. Y4C for short, he said, how's that sound? Wicked, eh?

I said it was the stupidest name I'd ever heard.

I said I hate you Jordan Yale.

He said not to call him Jordan anymore. He was now going by Youth.

He said he'd already figured out my Y4C name too. It was easy. I should just shorten my name, Harmony, to Harm.

I said no. No way. Never, never, never will I join Youth 4 Crime or call myself Harm.

By the next weekend he was with Christine, who now calls herself Crime. So much for the best friends forever thing. I've never spoken to either of them again. And whenever

I see Christine/Crime or Jordan/Youth at school, it's like we're invisible to each other.

By mid-November I'd missed my period. No matter how many times I got out a calendar and recounted the days, I was still late. And since that had never happened before I was beginning to figure out why. I knew I might be pregnant. It was impossible and unbelievable and I was so, so scared. In December my breasts started aching and I threw up every morning. I threw up every afternoon and in the evenings too. I wanted to sleep all the time. I couldn't stand the smell of food, so I stopped eating dinner.

I didn't know what to do or where to turn, so I tried to hide everything from my parents and I waited. I waited in nauseous hope that I was wrong. I checked for blood a hundred times a day. And then I missed my next period. Of course my parents had figured out that something was going on. At first Mom thought I had an eating disorder. She confronted me one morning just before Christmas holidays. She was waiting for me outside the bathroom door when I came out. Harmony, she said, honey, were you vomiting in there? Because I'm sure I heard you, and every other morning this week too. Then she started blabbing on about anorexia and bulimia and how dangerous they are and how we could get help and work things out if I'd just talk to her.

I started to cry. I sobbed and sobbed and sobbed. She tried to hold me but I had to run back into the bathroom and hurl again. Mom followed, and when she saw I wasn't doing it on purpose, she gasped with shock. Oh. My. God. she said. You're pregnant!

I couldn't deny it.

How on earth did that happen? Mom wanted to know.

Really, Mom? The usual way, I said, which was mean because she was so upset and only wanted to help me. So then I told her the truth, which was that I didn't really know. And that I hated the guy, and that I didn't want to have a baby, and that this couldn't be happening to me.

But it was.

Mom said not to worry, that we could find a solution, and at first I was glad of her help. It was such a relief to have her take control. She bought me a pregnancy test kit and then she arranged an appointment with our family doctor. She came with me and held my hand. But then when we got home and sat down with Dad to decide what to do, I was sorry they'd ever found out. I wished I'd tried harder to hide my pregnancy from them. Because they started talking about "our" baby. And when I tried to discuss having an abortion, they wouldn't hear of it.

Please don't be offended, Rue. But I did think about abortion. A lot. I really, really, didn't want to do that, but it seemed like it might be for the best. I didn't feel ready to have a baby. I knew I wasn't mature enough to be a mother. It was my own fault of course, but I hadn't planned on having a baby and I really didn't want to be pregnant. And when I thought about what the world is like, with terrorism and wars and disease and poverty and global warming and all, it seemed like it would be better not to bring you into such a scary place.

But my parents, who have always been pro-choice, decided that in your case the choice was theirs, not mine. And they chose for me to go ahead with the pregnancy. They didn't pressure me into getting married or anything. I think they didn't want to have to share you with a husband/father who might stand up to them more than I would. Not that Jordan/Youth would have been into that anyway. But they did pressure me. They made a plan and pushed me into accepting it. I could complete my school year before giving birth and they'd help me raise you. They'd look after you during the days while I finished high school and whatever else. They'd see to everything. It was almost as if you were going to be their baby and I would be like a surrogate mother or something.

I knew my parents had wanted more children but started their family too late. By the time they had me they were in their forties and Mom couldn't get pregnant again. I knew they longed for grandchildren. I knew they'd look after us. And I was so ill and exhausted all the time that I let them wear me down. I let them talk me out of terminating the pregnancy. I also let them talk me out of even thinking about putting you up for adoption. Every time I tried to argue with them, they calmly showed me a way they could solve whatever problem I was worried about. They wanted me to have you so much that they made every other option feel wrong.

So I gave in and agreed to go along with their plan. And I started feeling a tiny bit of hope. It wasn't what I'd imagined for my life. But on days when I was able to keep food down and actually had enough sleep, I began to feel like things might be okay. Maybe even good. I could do this.

Hahahahaha. You hear that? That's the sound of the universe laughing.

Sorry Rue, I can't tell you anymore at the moment. Too painful. So let's talk about something else. Because one good thing did happen today. There's a new guy at school. I've seen him before, at the cemetery, every day over the long weekend. Okay, I watched his mother's funeral from behind a tree. It wasn't much of a funeral, just a burial really. And that was so distressing to me. There was just him, and his grandfather, and the cemetery caretaker. No brothers or sisters or aunts or uncles or friends of the family.

Of course everybody in Dunlane knows about this guy's mother getting killed in an accident and all. There was an article about her in the paper with a photo of her as Miss Dunlane 1996. The photo showed her riding in a convertible in the Canada Day parade and she looked so pretty. She also looked so young. She must have been a teenager when she had him. I guess she made some mistakes too. That picture and the story about her accident really upset me.

Anyway, when I saw this guy at the cemetery, it's the first time I've felt even halfway happy for months. I almost didn't care that he was, you know, a *grieving teen* like me. Someone I'd normally avoid like an STI. And actually, my first thought when I saw him was to run away. He looked so sad and scared and lost. And I don't need that. I've got a lifetime supply of my own sorrow to deal with already.

But he's sooooo hot! He's tall, with longish, dark hair and I was really hoping he'd be going to DDHS. I was super thrilled to see him there today. But too bad for him, Youth and Crime must have seen him at the cemetery too, because they already paid him a locker visit after school. And now they've got everybody calling him Ghoul Guy.

His real name is Liam.

Hey, I just thought of something. Maybe Liam's going to that support group Sarita wants me to join. I don't want anybody's help, but I wouldn't mind helping him. If I could. I know I said I wasn't interested in other teens with grief issues. But I'd make an exception for him. I don't know why, but I just get this hopeful feeling when I see him. A feeling like maybe the world isn't such a bad place after all.

So far he's not hanging with Y4C. At least I don't think he was part of that swarming on Main Street. I'd like to warn him about joining them, because if he did, that would ruin everything.

Fog

By Saturday morning after his first week at DDHS, Liam can't stay away from the cemetery any longer. He misses his mom too much. She'll be wondering why he hasn't shown up. Why he's left her there beside her mother where she definitely does not want to be.

Who cares what happens with Youth and Crime? Don't be a wimp, his mom would say. So he's going to visit her grave.

He heads for the cemetery early, while Gully's still sleeping. Lucky him, able to sleep late. Sleep is Liam's only escape these days, but it never comes soon enough or lasts long enough. And waking up is terrible, because for the first few seconds he forgets what's happened. He thinks he's home in Mr. Cash & Condo's place with his mom.

And then it all comes rushing back. A flood of sorrow swamps him like a rogue wave. The water rolls him over and over until he can't tell which way is up. Until he's drowning in grief.

When he finally surfaces, forcing himself out of bed, he can't get his bearings. Then he panics. Just like that time he and his mom went on holiday, when he got disoriented in the fog and couldn't find her.

For his twelfth birthday they'd taken a trip to the west coast. They wanted to go somewhere far away from the city, somewhere they'd never been. They wanted to see the mountains and ocean. So they flew to BC and booked into a lodge near Tofino on Vancouver Island. They hiked in the rainforest, sea kayaked, and even tried to surf. On the last day they were fogged in, but walked on the beach anyway.

It was weird, hearing the waves breaking but not being able to see out over the water or anywhere around them. Then suddenly Liam couldn't even see his mom.

She'd been right there, walking along the shoreline ahead of him. But then she was gone. Even her footprints were washed away.

He lost it and started to yell. *Mom! Mom! Where are you? Where are you?*

That's how he feels every day, every time he wakes up. Except that now he knows he won't eventually find his mom a little way up the beach, sitting on a big old cedar log. Looking like a little kid in the yellow raincoat the lodge lent her. That's the image he keeps in his mind though. He pictures her sitting there waving to him through the fog. Hears her calling, *It's okay, Liam. Everything's okay. I'm right here.*

Today the sun is shining and the sky is a cruel, clear blue. No fog at all, except in Liam's head. It's the kind of day he'd normally feel happy. If his mom hadn't been killed in a hit-and-run. If he hadn't been forced to live in DumpLane. And if he wasn't on his way to the cemetery, worried what a certain gang might do to him.

He's really hoping that Y4C partied all night and none of them will be awake yet. It's only nine o'clock, so he should be safe for at least an hour or so. But he keeps a careful watch as he walks along anyway. Just in case some of them stayed out all night and are only now staggering home.

Mount Hope & Glory Cemetery is seven blocks from Gully's house, right by the murky Ernest River that flows through the middle of town. The grounds look like a huge and welcoming park. Winding pathways lead through tall, leafy trees. The ornate gates in the black iron fence stand wide open. Liam starts to feel better as soon as he passes through them.

It's so peaceful here in the cemetery. Like he's stepped into another world. Which of course he has. He's entered a place where time stands still. Where everyday things don't matter.

The land of the dead.

Where his mom lives now.

Forever.

To get to her grave Liam has to cross the old part of the cemetery. It's the most park-like, hilly and quaint. Here the gravestones are all helter-skelter. They lean at odd angles and are so weathered he can hardly read the writing on them.

He can't help wondering about all those people from the past, now nothing but bones. What's the point of life on Earth anyway? And what happens after? He hates thinking about this stuff, but here in the cemetery it's hard to avoid.

There are some people wandering about, but they're not Y4C. Not with those geeky tourist hats and shoes and backpacks. He remembers that caretaker guy Pete going on about how Mount Hope & Glory Cemetery is on the town's historic walking tour. He said there are some unusual gravestones. And some famous folks—early politicians or something—are supposed to be buried here. But Liam can't remember who, and doesn't much care.

He hurries on to the new part of the cemetery, careful to check all around. Not that he's scared. He's just watching his back. He hears birds singing, but otherwise he seems to be alone. It's not likely the tourists will bother coming over here. This part of the cemetery is flat and treeless, the graves set in straight, bleak rows.

The soil is still mounded up over his mom's grave. It hasn't settled like it has over the older graves, and the grass seed hasn't sprouted yet. The wreath of pink roses and the baskets of sympathy flowers are faded and brown. He thinks about clearing them away, but hasn't the heart.

What would he do with them? Chuck them in the garbage? Maybe Gully or that caretaker guy will deal with them later. At least Liam brought fresh flowers, a bunch of lilacs he picked in Gully's yard.

He sits down by the Hall family's gravestone, placing the lilacs in front. The top of the stone is a polished pink granite rectangle, with butterflies and birds carved around the edges. The bottom is a rough grey block.

He wishes now that he'd argued with Gully about burying his mom here. How can she rest in peace if she's stuck in DumpLane's Mount Hope & Glory Cemetery, beside her hated mother?

But he was still in shock back when that decision was made. He was so glad to have Gully taking care of all the details. And although it bothers Liam, it does seem to comfort Gully that mother and daughter are reunited now. It's like he thinks they'll make up or something if they're forced to spend eternity together. He's had the new engraving done already:

Monica Susan Hall, 1979-2011
Dearly Beloved. Always Remembered.
Rest in Peace.

She was only thirty-two years old. When they went out for coffee or for dinner people always thought she was Liam's sister. Or sometimes even his date. She was way too young to die.

He slumps down onto the sorry pile of dirt that covers her grave. It's been days since he cried and he hoped he was done. But no such luck. And once he starts he can't seem to stop.

Why, why, why? Why'd she go out that night? She said she'd always be there for him. She promised!

He blubbers like a baby and lets the tears and snot stream down his face.

Until he realizes he's no longer alone. There's someone standing nearby. Someone from Y4C, for sure. Listening to him rave. Watching him do the ugly cry.

He rubs his eyes with his fists and wipes his nose with the back of his hand. Gross, but right now, who really cares? He sniffles and gulps some deep breaths and braces himself for what's coming.

Strangely, he's still not afraid. Bring it on, he wants to say. Beat me up like you did that little old lady. Kick my head in. C'mon, kill me already and get it over with. Because I don't care. My life is shit.

Nothing happens though. No fists in his face or boots to his head. So finally he glances up.

But it's not Youth or Crime or anybody looking like a 4 standing there. It's this girl. She's tall and slender and pale. Her hair is all wavy and shiny over her shoulders like a waterfall. Her feet are bare. She has silver rings on her toes and her toenails are painted a dark, winy red, like blood.

She swishes the skirt of her long, lime-green dress. It's some kind of a prom gown he guesses. "Hey," she says, sitting down beside him on his mom's grave. "Do you know how many dead babies are buried in this place?"

Dead babies? What's with this chick? He lifts the edge of his T-shirt to clean his face. There's tears and snot smeared all over him. He must look revolting. "No idea," he says. "Never even thought about it. I'm Liam, by the way."

"I know," she says. "I've seen you at school."

"You have?" So why hasn't he seen her? Because he would have noticed. For sure.

"I'm Harmony."

"Harmony. Nice name." Her hair is the most beautiful he's ever seen. It's the colour of honey. He'd like to touch it. Stroke it. Stuff it in his mouth. But he restrains himself. She'd probably freak. And he'd probably lose all control and ravish her. Which would definitely be a very bad move.

"The babies have to be under two years old for me to visit them," she says. "I bring them flowers. And other stuff too, like candles and charms."

Is she for real? Or is he hallucinating? Did she really just say what he thinks she did? "You visit the graves of dead babies?"

She nods, like that's the most natural thing in the world. "Some of them are over a hundred years old now. Well, they would be, if they'd lived."

He leans back against the gravestone. This Harmony chick seems a bit crazy. The last thing he needs is to get involved in a long conversation with a fruitcake, even if she is incredibly hot. "If you really want to know how many dead babies are here, you could just ask the caretaker guy. He's got stacks of old cemetery maps and records in his office.

"Yeah, right. Pete would chase me away and call the cops."

"Really? He seemed okay to me. But maybe he was just being nice when I met him, because he knows my grandfather."

"Probably," she says, "because trust me, he'd never let any other kid set foot in his office." She scowls in the direction of the caretaker's restored chapel office. "And I wouldn't go in there anyway." Liam gets the feeling she wants to say more but stops herself. "Besides, I like finding the babies' graves myself. I go to a different part of the cemetery every Saturday morning—that's the safest time."

"Safest?"

"Yeah, safest. See, there's some kids who hang out here. They get drunk and do drugs and vandalize stuff. Last Halloween there was a big party and they knocked down about fifty gravestones."

"I might have heard something about that."

"And did you hear about that swarming on Main Street the other day?"

"Oh man, that was terrible about that old lady." Liam still can't get the picture of her lying on the sidewalk out of his mind. Just like he can't delete the image of his mom lying in the road after her accident. Whoever was driving the car that hit her just took off and left her to die. How could they do that? Sure, sure, he didn't help that old lady, but he knew that somebody would. "You think it was the same kids?"

"I know it was."

"What a bunch of assholes." Yeah, right. And he's one too. He shouldn't have gone into the hardware store and pretended not to see that old lady. But at least he watched to make sure the ambulance came.

There was nobody to help his mom. The police said she probably died instantly. That she didn't feel a thing. But still. She was all alone.

"They call themselves Youth 4 Crime," Harmony says. "Y4C."

"Actually, I already met their leaders. First day of school."

"Now why doesn't that surprise me?" She swoops her breathtaking hair back off her heart-stopping face. "You don't want to mess with them."

"And you know this because?"

She looks like she's going to cry. Or run away. Or both. "I'm just saying."

"Uh-huh. So what's the story with them?"

Now she fiddles with her silver toe rings, moving them from one foot to the other. "Oh, you know—young and stupid and nothing else to do. Some are total losers, but some are good kids acting out for a laugh. And some are just spoiled brats who think they can do whatever they want." She bends towards him and moves his arm so she can read the gravestone. "That's your mother?"

He rubs the spot where this vision in lime green called Harmony touched his arm. "Yeah. How'd you know?"

"Well, you're new at school, and pretty much everybody knows why." Now Harmony busies herself rearranging the lilacs he brought. "Tell me about her?"

But before he can answer, she suddenly stops what she's doing and looks all around. "I can smell Y4C," she says. "We better bail."

Then he sees some kids lurking nearby. Where did they come from? He was so busy staring at Harmony that he forgot to keep watch. He forgot everything but her.

"They're 4s," Harmony says. "Spying for Youth and Crime. They must have slept here or something. We're screwed."

Choices

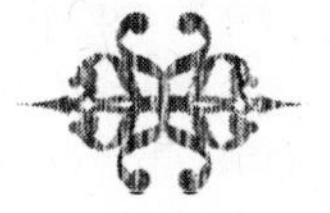

Hey Rue,

Awesome news! I'm so excited! I've met him! I've talked to Liam! Here's how it happened. You know how I always go to the cemetery on Saturday mornings? Well, he was there too, and our paths just kind of crossed by chance. Okay, okay, so it wasn't really a coincidence. I saw him come through the gates but he didn't see me, because I was pretending to read that historic sign that says how Mount Hope & Glory Cemetery was founded in 1868 or something as a final resting place for the early settlers. I stayed back while he looked around the old part of the cemetery for a bit, and then I followed him to the new part, where his mother is buried. Before I approached him I let him have some private time at her grave. Which he definitely needed because as soon as he got there he broke down and cried. Like really, really wept, making all these horrible gasping choking sounds. And in between he was raging too, yelling all this stuff to his mother like why, why, why and what was he supposed to do without her and so on.

I didn't want to interrupt and embarrass him, but I was getting concerned. I mean, if I didn't distract him, how else he was going to stop? And better me than some stupid Y4C.

What if one of them came along and heard him? That would be way worse.

I was wearing my current favourite dress, a metallic lime-green prom gown Mom saved from her high school days. She sewed it herself and it's got puffy Juliet sleeves and a fitted bodice and a long swirly skirt. God knows why Dazey bothered to keep it for forty years, but I'm glad she did because it's totally epic. Too bad she didn't also save the satin shoes she had dyed to match. But I don't really mind because I like going barefoot in the cemetery. The caretaker keeps the lawns so green and lush that I feel like I'm walking into a storybook. The velvety grass underfoot makes me want to dance around the mossy, old gravestones. And sometimes I do. I know that might sound freaky, but when I'm dancing in the cemetery I feel better, more connected to life, than I do at home or at school or any other time really. Then when I stop, I stand so still that I could grow roots and transform into one of those fairytale trees with a mournful face. The ones that live forever in haunted forests.

Anyway I didn't tell Liam about you, but I did tell him about visiting the dead babies' graves. I know it was risky. But I had to find out if that would scare him off. Because I do realize it's not a completely normal thing to do. He did seem kind of surprised, but he didn't run away from me or anything. Actually I think he's too sad about his mom dying to care very much about anything else. But I know he sort of liked me—I could tell by the way he looked at me. I'm not sure how I feel about that though, because the last time I thought a guy liked me, look what happened.

There was a bad moment when Liam said I should go ask the cemetery caretaker for records of all the dead babies. I had a flashback to Halloween when Jordan and I snuck into that restored chapel where the caretaker keeps those records and then I remembered how my purple princess dress was ruined, all ripped and stained and I had this weird feeling that I was going to remember all the nasty details of whatever we did. And I almost told Liam everything right then. But instead I just told him about Y4C and of course he'd already heard about the cemetery party and all the damage. I don't think he figured out that I was there. God, I hope he never does.

And then we ran because some of them were watching us. Which proves they are after him. I so hope he's careful about Y4C. They are bad, bad news. They're going to try to suck him into their gang and destroy his life. I know because that's what happened to me. I hung out with them once. Just one stupid night. And now I'm nuts.

Anyway, what I told you before, about my parents talking me into keeping you? Well just so you know, I want to clarify that it's not that I didn't want you, it's that you came along too soon. Like at least ten or maybe even fifteen years too soon. I always planned to have children someday. Just not in high school, you know? And I kept remembering that thing we had to do in Family Studies where we carried a baby doll around for a week and had to look after it and how hard that was. And that was just a freaking doll, not a real live crying puking pissing crapping baby like you would have been. Please believe me.

I was terrified!

So after a few weeks of being pregnant I told Mom I'd changed my mind about our plan. I'd begun to worry that if anything ever happened to my parents, I'd be stuck on my own with you. Mom's fifty-eight and Dad's sixty-three, and you just never know. They could have heart attacks and die, or get Alzheimer's or cancer or something. I might have to look after them, and how would I do that if I had a baby to care for too? So even though it was almost too late to have an abortion, and I didn't want to choose that option anymore anyway, I tried to bring up adoption again. It seemed like a good idea to me. Especially since I'd read about open adoptions, where the birth mother chooses the adoptive parents and has a relationship with her child, like an aunt or something. I knew there were lots of couples who couldn't have children and were just waiting for a sweet little baby like you. Young couples, who wouldn't be in their seventies and all decrepit when you were a teenager, like Mom and Dad would. And who'd be okay with the idea of me visiting you and being part of your life.

But ohmigod, Mom went bonkers when I mentioned adoption again. I have never, ever, ever, not even when she first realized I was pregnant, seen her so upset. It took awhile, but finally she confessed why. It turns out there's a deep dark secret in her past. Something life changing she hadn't told me before. Oh yeah, and she'd never told Dad either. So you can see we were both a bit shocked to find out she'd had a baby when she was sixteen. Which to be fair was years before she even met Dad. But still. She said she gave this baby, a boy, by the way, up for adoption and she's regretted that decision ever since. There was a lot of crying and hugging and carrying on.

You mean to tell me, Mom, I said, that I have a half-brother out there somewhere who is, like, over forty years old? That's right, she said. And then she went on and on about how she thought she'd have years ahead of her to have millions of babies and then it turned out that by the time she got around to trying she was too old and she couldn't conceive again after she had me. And now she's so sorry not to have kept him, her first dear little baby, or told anybody about him, or ever tried to find him. She never held him or even saw him, because back in those days they didn't let unwed mothers giving babies up for adoption make any kind of bond in case they changed their minds. She named him Lakefield for his father, who she never told, and never kept in touch with, but who went to some private school with that name. She didn't know where her baby would be placed or who his adoptive family would be. So she tried her best to let him go. To let him have the life she couldn't give him at the time.

So will you look for him now? I asked because I think she should.

No. She will not. More bawling. Lots more bawling. And who can blame her for crying over him? When she calmed down she said Lakefield probably isn't even called that anymore and he has other parents and she respects their privacy. She only told me about him so I'd realize how great it is that I have choices. Apparently way back last century when girls "got in trouble" they had to have illegal backstreet abortions that usually killed them or else they had to go hide in shame in a home for unwed mothers, which is what she did. And then as I said they had to give their baby up without ever holding it or even seeing it. And when they came home with the made-up story that they'd been staying with their grandmother or their aunt they were social outcasts with a ruined reputation, because everyone knew where they'd been anyway. They were considered damaged goods, and nobody wanted to marry them. So I am very lucky that today I can go ahead and have a baby without all that shame and scandal, and with the benefit of provincial health coverage and also my parents' complete support.

Awesome! Who knew getting pregnant was such a good deal for a fifteen-year-old these days? More girls should get into it and live their mother's dream of keeping their unplanned babies. Okay, yeah, I know that's harsh. But it's not my fault if Mom has never forgiven herself for giving up Lakefield, and saw you as her chance to make good, or her chance to have the babies she never had. If she really cares about her lost baby she should find him and apologize and get over it. Really.

But after that I kind of gave up on the adoption thing. Mom was so obsessed and emotional about it that I couldn't fight her. It was as if I only had the energy and strength to grow you, and I had to let her deal with everything else. And once we'd decided for the second time against adoption, I went back to being fully committed to having you and raising you with my aged parents, no matter what happened.

So far I have never told anybody but my parents about you. Mom and Dad talked to me about telling Jordan/Youth. They said he had a right to know. Mom said she regrets keeping Lakefield a secret from his father, and doesn't want me to make the same mistake. But I refused. And not because I thought that Jordan/Youth wouldn't care. It was because I didn't want to take the chance of him ever having anything to do with you. I couldn't face you having visits with a guy I hated and hearing you call him Daddy. It was completely and utterly selfish and wrong, I know. But I needed to feel like I had some control over what was happening to me. And I also didn't want Christine/Crime to find out who my baby's father was. I was still so hurt by her setting me up at that party so she could have Jordan for herself. And I figured she'd be mad and jealous that I was having her boyfriend's baby and spread more ugly rumours about me being a slut or something. But more than that, she'd somehow find a way to ruin your birth and mess up your start in life.

In the end my parents were just as glad to leave your father out of it. They were conflicted at first because they believed he had rights, but they wanted to respect my decision not to inform him. So to ease their minds I told them about Jordan changing his name to Youth, and some of the stuff he got kids to do. How bad a father he'd make. And they sure didn't want the leader of Youth 4 Crime anywhere near their precious grandbaby. In fact they wanted to turn him in to the police. They wanted him punished for his involvement in the cemetery vandalism and also for what he'd done to me. But I talked them out of it because I didn't want the publicity. I didn't want anybody to know anything about what had happened.

If I get close to Liam, I might tell him about you. If it seems like he can handle the truth. Because if we're going to have a relationship, I want to be completely honest with him. I don't want you to be a secret between us.

If we have a relationship? What am I thinking? Liam's a grieving teen and I'm a loony nutbar. Does that sound like a good combination?

Tomatoes

Harmony, Harmony, Harmony. When Liam gets home from the cemetery she's all he can think about. Well, almost all. Because his mom is never not in his mind. She's like a tissue of thought that's always with him. But today the fog keeps closing in around his picture of her, making it harder and harder to see her face. And instead of a beach and a log and a yellow raincoat, he keeps seeing the cemetery and a gravestone and the girl of his dreams in a lime-green prom dress.

He's a teenage guy after all. So it's probably normal to be obsessed with Harmony, even though his mom's just died. At least he hopes it is. And he knows his mom would like her. She'd want him to be friends with her and not feel guilty about getting on with his life. She believed in living in the now. And in Liam's now, he's just met a strange but beautiful girl. And he can't wait to see her again.

That afternoon Gully asks Liam if he wants come to a garden centre out in the country. He says it's time to get this year's tomato plants to put in tomorrow. And since it's such a nice day and Liam can't stand to stay in the house, he agrees to go along.

Gully chooses an old Eagles CD for them to listen to on the ride. Not what Liam would pick, but Gully didn't ask. And yet it feels like the right music for an old guy and his teenage grandson, riding in a pickup on this late spring Saturday.

Gully shifts gears smoothly as they drive with the windows wide open and the music cranked loud over the sound of the V8 engine. They don't want or need to talk. It's enough just to be going somewhere.

It's crazy busy at Growing Green Gardens, even though it's way north of the highway and takes almost an hour to get to. Gully says that's because they have the best quality nursery stock, and they specialize in heirloom vegetable varieties you can't find anywhere else.

They buy four each of seven different kinds of tomatoes, so they'll have a crop ready to pick from early summer until late fall. And they'll have all sizes from those little tiny ones for salads to huge beefsteak ones for slicing up for burgers. Seems like a lot of tomatoes, but what does Liam know?

He'd rather think about Harmony.

After they drop the plants off at home they go out for pizza. At the restaurant they see some guys Gully works with, celebrating winning a baseball tournament. But when Gully introduces him their smiles disappear. They look at Liam the same way that cemetery caretaker Pete did the day of his mom's burial. Embarrassed and sorry and awkward. He's sure they all know what happened to his mom and why Gully suddenly has a grandson living with him.

But somehow today that kind of reaction doesn't bother Liam. He's hanging with his grandfather, who everybody likes. Gully's got friends. He's got respect.

And this morning Liam met Harmony.

After the pizza they go see a movie. This time Gully does ask what he'd like, so Liam picks the latest Swedish thriller, because he guesses that's what Gully's hoping for. Gully's a huge fan. As they wait in the lineup he raves about the first movies in the series.

Liam doesn't much care about the plot details, but like the Eagles music in the truck, it gives them something to focus on.

So he listens to Gully, happy to be out doing something, not sitting home alone. Happy to not have to talk about his mom, or how much they both miss her.

On Sunday morning Liam's digging twenty-eight holes in Gully's garden. It's cloudy, which Gully declares perfect for planting, but hot. Why'd he bother taking a shower before he started this? He's already soaked with sweat and covered with dirt. "What exactly are we going to do with all the tomatoes?" he asks, stopping a minute to rest. "Aren't there going to be way too many?"

"No such thing as too many tomatoes," Gully says. "Think about toasted tomato sandwiches with bacon and mayo. Tomato, basil and mozzarella salad. Fresh salsa." He sets out the little plants beside the holes Liam's dug. "I freeze some of them for making tomato sauce in the winter. And I take some to folks at work. Everybody loves them. You'll see. You've never tasted anything so good."

"Huh. Killer tomatoes, eh?"

Gully laughs. "That's what they say."

Beside the plants Gully also has ready twenty-eight old hockey sticks with the blades cut off, and twenty-eight large juice cans with both ends gone. "What's with all that stuff?"

"The sticks are to stake the plants later. But we put them in now." Gully adds something called bone meal to the first hole before gently setting in a tomato plant. He fills in around it with the soil Liam dug out earlier. Then he pats it down gently, like he's tucking in a newborn baby or something. "After we get them all planted and watered," he says, "we put the cans around them for the first while. Keeps them safe from cutworm." He lifts his straw gardening hat to wipe his forehead with the back of his hand.

It's so weird, suddenly having a grandfather. Especially since Liam never had a father. "Man, you really love your garden."

Something is making him want to connect with Gully. Must be all that male bonding yesterday.

"It's my therapy," Gully says. "And with a job like mine, I sure need it. I spend way too much time in that shithole prison."

Liam hands him the next plant. "I heard that the guards there are always finding homemade weapons, like shivs from filed down toothbrushes and stuff."

Gully adds bone meal and sets the plant in place without looking at him. "You heard?" He fills in the soil and pats it down. "Heard where?"

"You know, at school. Lots of kids' parents work at the prison too."

Gully points to the area where he planted his tomatoes last year. He's already explained how he has to plant them in a different place every season. "Peas, beans, carrots," he says. "That's what we'll put over there. When your Mom was a kid she used to like to plant radishes. They only take about three weeks." He strips off his T-shirt and throws it to the ground. "Getting a bit warm, isn't it?"

For somebody over sixty, Gully's in great shape. The guy's ripped. His shoulders and chest are massive. "You ever confiscate any homemade weapons?" Liam asks. "You ever been in a riot?"

Gully swears under his breath and stops working. "Look Liam," he says. "Working at the prison is a steady job with a good pension. I'm a supervisor. I've got another three years till I retire. And that's all I'm ever going to tell you. I absolutely refuse to talk about that place. So please don't ask." He fiddles with a plant he's already finished patting down, loosening the soil and straightening the stalk a bit. "You got that?"

"Sorry." Liam goes to fill the watering cans. Gully likes the new plants watered by hand, not with the hose. Better for the roots or something. When he comes back Liam says, "Remember how I said that Mom used to tell me about your garden?"

That stops Gully. He freezes in place, like they're playing that statues game. Liam waits. Silence. Then Gully acts busy with his trowel. He scrapes one of the holes deeper. Liam watches sweat trickle down his muscular back. "She said that helping you was really special to her."

He waits again, but Gully still doesn't speak. Plant, fill, pat down. He keeps going with his tomatoes. Okay, more pressure. "And she told me once that you planted a tree for her, when she was born."

"That's right," Gully finally mutters. "At our old house. Planted another one for her when I moved here. That flowering crabapple in the front yard."

"Really?" She never told him about the second tree. But then maybe she didn't know. "You mean the one covered with all those pink flowers?"

Gully nods.

"It's beautiful."

Gully nods again and points to an evergreen by the far fence. "Planted that blue spruce for you."

He did? "Hey, I never knew that." It's not a huge tree, only about as tall as Liam. But it's a cool silvery-blue colour, and perfectly shaped. It looks like something you'd see on a Christmas card, the branches topped with fluffy snow. And underneath there'd be some woodland creatures looking up at a night sky shining with stars and a full moon.

"Well, I told your mother about it," Gully says. "*She* knew. Same thing as her tree—I'd planted one for you at the old house when you were born, so when I moved here I planted another one."

Liam feels like he's been stabbed by one of those homemade prison weapons. "Well, I guess there's lots of stuff she didn't tell me," he says, wondering why Miss Dunlane 1996 didn't bother to tell him about his tree. Sure, she didn't like to talk about the past, but she did talk about Gully and his gardening.

"I meant it when I asked her to come back home, you know." Gully reaches for his T-shirt to wipe the sweat off his torso. "Well, the both of you. Especially after her mother died. But I couldn't convince her. So I just kept sending her money."

"You sent money?" Liam never knew that, either. And it can't be true. "But Mom always said that she did, you know, *what she did*, to support us." More stabbing pain in his heart. Thanks a lot, Mom.

Is it possible to bleed to death from emotional pain? Gully sent money and she didn't even bother to mention it? This is way worse than her not telling him that she was Miss Dunlane. "She said she couldn't make enough at anything else."

Gully picks up his trowel, throws it down again and sits back on his heels. He looks Liam in the eye. Then he shakes his head like he's got bees in his ears or something. "Time to grow up, boy. She didn't have to do *that*. It was her choice."

"*What*?" Did he really say it was her choice? "What do you mean?"

"Just that," Gully says. "She had choices. I made sure of it."

"But," Liam says. And then he can't think of anything to add. Because if what Gully says is true, then his mom deliberately lied to him. A lot. And he can't face that.

He just stands there feeling stunned and betrayed. Finally he says, "There must be some mistake."

"The lilacs will soon be done," Gully answers, pointing to a forest of bushes across the back of the yard. They've been in full bloom all week.

"Hey, please don't change the subject. We were talking about my mom."

"I know. And I think we should both focus on our good memories of her. And one of mine is that she loved lilacs. We had a lot at the old house, and they're one reason I bought this place." He stands and stretches his back, brushes the dirt off his hands. "She used to say that lilacs looked like purple clouds and they smelled like heaven."

"Oh," Liam says. "Well, I picked some for her grave."

"I know. I saw them there, at the cemetery." Gully looks like he's going to say something more. But then he stops himself. "I'm ready for a break. Think I'll go make some coffee. You want anything? Cold drink?"

"Nah, I'm okay." Liam's not okay, not anywhere near. But he wants to stay out here with the lilacs. "I'll keep working."

His mom really loved flowers. She used to say that if she ever had a straight job it would be as a florist, so she could work with flowers every day. She used to buy them for herself at Sprigs & Twigs, the flower shop on the corner, every week, just to make their place look nice.

The only flowers she didn't like were the fancy bouquets of a dozen red roses that sometimes got delivered to their door. She always threw those in the garbage. Even if they came from Mr. Cash & Condo.

She had a rule that she never accepted flowers from clients. Gifts, yes. Jewellery mostly. Sometimes fancy clothes or wine or chocolates. Sports tickets—always the best seats in the Rogers or Air Canada Centre—from Mr. Cash & Condo. And the condo itself, of course.

But that was only because Mr. Cash & Condo wanted to marry her and have them all live there together someday. Like after he got a divorce. Talking about that always made her laugh and say it would never happen, but if it did she'd make good on her side of the deal.

She'd give up being an escort and be his wife. But meanwhile, she said, they should enjoy living the good life. They should spend Mr. Cash & Condo's money. Good thing they did, before she died and he kicked Liam out.

A tapping on Gully's wooden fence brings Liam back to the present. He peeks through the slats. Surprise, surprise. It's Youth and Crime. Who knows how long they've been lurking there.

"Open the gate, Ghoul Guy," Youth says. "We wanna talk to you."

Crime adds, "Yeah. Open up or we'll kick it in."

Liam goes and unlatches the gate.

Youth sticks his head into the yard. "Been helping Gramps, eh?" he says. "Bet he'd be real upset if anything happened to his veggie garden."

Crime gives a deep, throaty laugh. "Bet he'd be real upset if he found all those poor little plants got ripped out in the night."

They wouldn't.

They would.

"Heard you were at the cemetery again this morning," Youth says. "How stupid are you, anyways? Or do you have a death wish like your *ho* of a mommy?"

Liam lunges at Youth, fists raised. But before he makes contact they all hear a door opening. Gully's coming back outside.

Youth and Crime saunter away. "We know where you live, Ghoul Guy."

Fetus

Hey Rue,

It's Sunday night and I'm so bored. I wonder what Liam is doing? I wonder if he's thinking about me? Or if he's missing his mother so much that he can't think of anything else? Ohmigod, how can he bear losing her? I'm not speaking to my own mom much, but it's hard to imagine not having her around. And it's totally impossible to imagine her dying. I'm not sure I could go on living if anything ever happened to her. No wonder Liam seems so sad and lonely and lost. I sure hope he hasn't gone back to the cemetery tonight. He really shouldn't risk letting Y4C see him there like I did yesterday, crying on his mother's grave.

I'm going to find Liam at school tomorrow and let him know I'd like to be his friend—maybe even more than that. Yeah, yeah, I'm probably thinking about Liam way too much. But it's such a relief that I'm not obsessing about Jordan/Youth all the time anymore. And even though I hate him, and I hate how he treated me, well, there's still something about him, you know? When I watch him with Christine/Crime around school, I can understand why she's attracted to him. He's hot in a perverted kind of way, like a con man in a movie. Somehow he makes you want to do whatever he says, even when you know you'll be sorry.

Sorry, sorry, sorry, sorry, sorry!

But enough about guys. I'm supposed to be writing down how I feel about you. So where was I? Pregnant and going along with my parents' plan to help me raise you. What was I thinking? you might wonder. It's okay, I wonder that all the time now. But I didn't back then. I guess it's one of those seemed-like-a-good-idea-at-the-time kind of things. I really believed it was the best solution for everyone. So by Christmas, Mom and Dad and I had pretty much accepted the situation and we were working as a team to provide you with the best possible prenatal experience.

Besides me taking multi-vitamins and avoiding stress and trying to eat and sleep well, your prenatal package included Noodle playing old '60s music he thought you needed to hear for an hour each evening, and then Dazey placing her hands on my belly and talking calmly to you about how much you were wanted and how great your life was going to be. Yeah, it was weird. Totally. But I was so overwhelmed by the whole pregnancy thing that the entire world felt weird. Everything was surreal and seemed to be happening to some other girl, not me.

We decorated the house for Christmas in our usual way, with lots of candles and cedar roping and a twelve-foot fir tree laden with Mom's collection of antique glass ornaments. One good thing about living in a historic house is that if you like to celebrate Christmas in the old-fashioned, pioneer way, which we do, then it's the perfect setting. Mom even made you a patchwork stocking. We hung it on the mantle and on Christmas morning it was full of useful presents for you: board books and bibs and non-toxic teething rings and organic baby bath products. While I stared at these, unsure what to do with them, Mom and Dad talked on about how this time next year you'd be about six months old, smiling and sitting up and learning to crawl.

On New Year's Eve, when most teens were out partying, I stayed home. My parents invited me to watch old movies with them. They had a wood fire going and a bowl of homemade caramel corn ready. But I needed to be alone. I took some popcorn and a mug of hot apple cider up to my room, where I put on the plaid flannel nightgown I got for Christmas. It looked matronly and childish, but I was finding pjs so uncomfortable, too tight and binding around the waist. The nightgown was soft and comfy and hung loose over my rounding belly. I lit some candles and climbed into bed with one of my other Christmas presents—a new fantasy novel. And then I lost myself in the story of a brave girl living in another world and time. A monstrous world where many scary and bad things happened, but where good conquered evil in the end.

For all of New Year's Eve, I let myself believe in magic. I made a resolution to stay strong and positive in the New Year, even though my life was going to be full of challenges. Then I snuggled under my quilt and dropped off to sleep full of hope for my future. I figured I could somehow cope with being pregnant, giving birth and being a mother. I only wished I had some supernatural powers like the girl in the book. Or any power at all, really.

Around the end of January, which according to the book on pregnancy and childbirth Mom bought me was the end of my first trimester, you were no longer an embryo but now something called a fetus. The illustration in the book showed a curled-up form with a huge head, kind of like a human bean sprout. And just like the book said, about this time I finally stopped being sick every day and exhausted every minute. I still had to pee all the time, but my breasts stopped hurting so much. They didn't stop getting bigger though, so Mom took me to Sears to buy some new, more supportive bras. Ew. It was so, so embarrassing that I made Mom pretend the bras were for her when we went into the change room.

Then I made her buy me a large, strawberry-mango smoothie and a toasted and buttered bagel, because now that I was feeling better I craved fruit and carbs. And ice cream. Loads and loads of ice cream. So we stopped at the dairy store on the way home to stock up on several flavours to keep on hand in the freezer for me. I could eat as much ice cream as I wanted, Mom said, because of the calcium. She'd been super nice to me since I decided to go along with her baby plan and I sometimes wondered if she was feeling guilty over convincing me to have you. Like she could make it okay by buying me whatever I wanted, which used to be against her principles. But I never came right out and asked her. I guess I didn't really want to know the answer.

Here's another thing that puzzled me. Nobody at school guessed I was pregnant. You were my little secret. Even back when I was throwing up all the time, nobody guessed you were morphing from an embryo into a fetus in my womb. Maybe it was because of my former Ice Queen Supreme reputation. Who would ever suspect that Harmony never-sees-anybody-more-than-two-weeks Trahern would even dream of doing something that could lead to having a baby? Or maybe it was because it's pretty normal to puke in the girls' washrooms. Everybody thinks, just like Mom did, that you're doing it on purpose because you're anorexic or bulimic or something. A couple girls from grade twelve even tried to share weight loss tips with me.

By sixteen weeks, which was near the end of February, I still wasn't showing yet. It was strange walking around school with you silently growing inside me. But being tall and bony, the ten pounds I'd already put on didn't make me look fat, more like maybe I was wearing an over-padded bra. Mom said with a first baby you don't look pregnant right away. She said she was able to hide her unplanned teenage pregnancy for almost five months by wearing a girdle! I'm not sure if they still sell girdles, but I did think about getting one of those Lycra bodyshaper things to wear under my clothes. Please don't think I was trying to hide you, but I didn't want to make a public announcement either. I wanted to keep you a secret as long as possible. Everybody would find out one way or another soon enough.

I wondered a lot about how kids would react when they did figure things out. Especially Christine/Crime. She'd freak for sure. But would anybody else care at all? It's not like I'd be the first unmarried teen at DDHS to have a baby. Lots of girls are finishing high school with a little kid—there's even an onsite daycare centre for staff and students. And it wasn't like I'd be shunned or anything. That had happened after the Halloween party in the cemetery last fall. I was already a girl to avoid in case my craziness was contagious. So the main problem would be whether Christine/Crime would guess who your father was. And when she did, which was inevitable, because she's not as stupid as she acts, would she tell him? Seeing as how he was now her boyfriend and all. And then what? Would I have to deny everything and make up some fake father? Would there be DNA tests and court custody battles?

It was all too bizarre to think about. So what I did instead was try really hard to keep up with my schoolwork. I had to focus on something, and I knew I still had to graduate and go to college or university so I could get a good job and support you and pay my parents back. Some days I could almost pretend my life was going to be normal again, that once I got through being a surrogate mother for my parents I'd be kind of like your older sister or your aunt or something. Honestly, to hear Dazey and Noodle making their lists of what they'd need—diapers, sleepers, car seat, sling, crib—and their plans to redo the guest bedroom upstairs, you'd think they were the expectant couple. Then they'd see me standing there, listening, and say oh Harmony, sweetie, what do you think? Spring green or buttercup yellow for the nursery walls?

Mom started making you a quilt, using scraps of fabric from dresses she'd sewn for me when I was little. Dad started refinishing an antique maple cradle. I started doing pelvic stretching and strengthening exercises from that book Mom gave me so I'd have an easier labour. Because after my doctor's appointment where I heard your heartbeat for the first time, which was the most shocking and also the most amazing sound I've ever heard, I realized in a new and very scary way that you were eventually going to be born. My body was somehow going to open up and push you out. The physical reality of that horrified me. It was going to hurt like hell and I didn't see how I'd ever be able to do it.

But back before that, Dr. Wembley, our family GP who'd delivered me and been my doctor ever since, had said I needed to make a birth plan. Although she'd keep seeing me for a couple more months, for the actual birth, I'd need someone else, as she didn't deliver babies anymore. So did I want a midwife or an obstetrician? A natural birth or pain management drugs? And what about feeding you? Breast or bottle? Breast was recommended, but I should consider how hard breastfeeding would be while going to school. I'd have to pump milk every day for Mom to feed you when I was in class. And so on.

I went home determined to figure out fast what I wanted to do. But after spending hours online here's what

I found out about pregnancy and birthing: there's way too much information out there! The more I read and researched, the more terrified I got. There is just so much that can go wrong.

In early March I went for a second trimester ultrasound so Dr. Wembley could check how big you were and that everything was normal, since you were now developing your vital organs. Mom went with me to the clinic. They made me drink so much water I thought I'd burst and then they wouldn't let me pee until after the test. Apparently a full bladder somehow helps make the ultrasound picture clearer.

The technician spread gel on my belly and pressed this thing that reminded me of a wand or something and is actually called a transducer over and over my skin while the computer beeped. While she was doing it I was able to watch the monitor to see your image and that was totally incredible, even better than hearing your heartbeat. I made a gasping sound because I was so shocked to actually see you and you kind of looked like a squiggly space alien surrounded by intergalactic light. Then I said out loud how beautiful you were and I started to laugh with the joyous emotion of it all and then Mom was sniffling and wiping away tears and I was sobbing my head off.

The technician said I'd have to wait to get the results at my next doctor's appointment but that everything looked fine and I was about nineteen weeks along. She reminded us in a calm but firm voice that a normal ultrasound does not guarantee a normal baby. And then she said that you were probably a girl, but there are always surprises.

Like, duh, I wanted to say. I almost told her that actually, you were already a surprise. But I think she kind of knew that.

Then she printed out your picture, called a sonogram, in black and white. Your very first photo. We rushed home to show it to Dad before Mom dropped me off at school for the rest of the day. I had math and history tests I didn't want to miss that afternoon.

Later that night I stuck your photo up on the fridge with a magnet from the health clinic. I tucked you in between my parents' two weekly lists. Their job list said: order crib and change table, prime nursery walls, pick up paint. Their shopping list said: cheese, lettuce, oranges, milk.

You looked so cute right there in the middle, where Mom used to display my artwork and school photos. And then I had this shocking flash-forward to the future, imagining myself putting your artwork in that space, along with family pictures of birthdays and holidays.

Who knew the sonogram would be your only photo.

Rage

Gully doesn't believe in dishwashers. He says they waste hot water and hydro. They're not eco-friendly. Not green. So he washes the dishes by hand in biodegradable, phosphate-free detergent. Most stuff he leaves to air-dry. But he wipes the cutlery with a clean dishtowel so there won't be any streaks.

Instead of pointing out the waste of human labour, and clipping ads for energy-efficient dishwashers from the Sears flyer, Liam helps him, every night. Not because he likes washing dishes. And not because he wants to be nice. He just hopes they can talk more about his mom.

Why wouldn't she let Gully help her? Why take his money but not his emotional support? Gully's an okay guy. Really. Liam's come to like him a lot. So what was her problem? Even if she couldn't get on with her mother, she could have had a relationship with her father. And Liam could have had a grandfather fifteen years sooner.

He'd also like to know why his mom always said she needed to work harder to earn more. Because Gully's confirmed that she cashed the cheques he sent her every month. He even showed Liam some old bank statements to prove it. So what did she do with the money?

Okay, he's pretty sure she didn't drink or smoke or snort it. No matter what else she did, his mom wasn't into any of that.

She looked after her health and worked out at a gym to keep fit. She ate her fruits and veggies and whole grains. She was a vegetarian, for god's sake. Sure, she liked a glass of wine, but she never over-indulged. Substance abuse was not part of her lifestyle.

She did like shoes though. When they moved to Mr. Cash & Condo's condo she had special shelving built for the walk-in closet in the master bedroom. Just to hold her shoe collection. When it was finished and she'd unpacked everything, she called Liam to come have a look.

It felt like going to the opening of a special exhibit at an art gallery or museum. There were rows and rows of shoes. Shiny, sexy, high-heeled shoes. Red, pink, purple, green, gold, silver, black. And boots too. Lots of high tight boots. And then she told Liam how much some of them cost. More than his trendiest sneakers. More than a month's groceries at the organic food store. More than a thousand bucks.

His mom was also fond of going to the beauty salon and spa. She was always getting her nails done or having her hair highlighted or her body waxed. Then there were massages, skin scrubs and facial treatments. And she did get breast implants a couple years ago. And other stuff, like Botox, that she didn't even need. All that costs. But his mom claimed she had to keep the tools of her trade in good working order. She had to spend money to stay looking young and hot.

But Gully never mentions her when they're doing the dishes. Talking about his daughter seems to be more difficult for Gully since he told Liam about the money thing. And no matter how many knives and forks and spoons Liam dries, he can't ask. The right questions just won't come out. So they talk about sports. The weather. The garden.

Mostly the garden. Always the tomatoes. Gully explains about organic methods of pest management, proper watering techniques, the benefits of mulching, when to pinch off the suckers, how to avoid blossom-end rot and hornworms.

And then the dishes are done.

One night Gully does say something different as he wipes down the counter. "Want a game of cards?"

Liam shuts the cutlery drawer. He hangs the dishtowel up to dry. He doesn't want to hurt Gully's feelings. But he hates cards.

Back when he was nine or ten, he spent way too many hours playing solitaire. Hours when his mom was working as an exotic dancer. That was before they got a computer. Once he could play video games and online poker, he shredded every pack of cards they owned. Too many bad memories.

He pictures himself as a kid home alone all evening wishing his mom was there. Watching the clock and counting the hours. Picturing his mom dancing—exotic dancing for money—as he deals another round of solitaire.

So yeah, he hates cards. But he says, "Okay." Maybe doing something more fun than dishwashing together will make Gully open up. "You'll have to teach me though." Strange as it sounds, he's never played cards with another person. Not even his mom. "I've only ever played online."

Gully shuffles and deals like a pro. "In the winter me and some of the guys from work have a regular poker game," he says. "First Friday of the month. You can come along. Hey, don't tell me what you've got."

Liam arranges the cards in his hand. "I didn't say anything."

"Your face," Gully says. "Keep it straight."

They play for an hour or so. That is, Gully deals some hands so he can explain stuff to Liam. But he's so caught up in passing on his poker expertise that they don't talk about anything else. Finally he yawns and says, "Okay, that's it for me. I'm going to bed."

Liam's not tired so he goes outside. He sits by the lilac bushes along the back fence, thinking about his mom. Thinking about her sitting in Gully's garden as a little girl. Thinking about her sitting on that beach log, fading into the mist.

Where are you, Mom? Where are you?

He knows some people would say she's in hell, suffering eternal damnation for her sins. And others would say she's forgiven, she's in heaven watching over him. He doesn't believe either is true. He just misses her. And he wishes he'd asked her a whole lot more questions.

When Liam was a baby they'd lived on social assistance. Then when he went to school, his mom worked as a waitress during the day. Nights she had a second job she could do from home. Phone-sex chat lines. Then she got into exotic dancing, because of the tips. That's how she met Laverne. Then they both got into the game on the side, for the extra money.

And then, when Liam was twelve, after they came back from their trip out west, she and Laverne started Arabella Investments. She called it a step up the career ladder. The road to financial security.

A year later, his mom met Mr. Cash & Condo. Who said he didn't want them living in a crappy apartment anymore. Who said he wanted to marry her. Who said he'd look after her kid, too. Who changed his mind when she died and didn't want anything to do with Liam.

If only she hadn't gone out that night. Liam and his mom were supposed to go to a movie together. But Mr. Cash & Condo called. The only client she'd break a date with her son for. Maybe she had to do what Mr. Cash & Condo said because of living in his place? Or maybe she really cared about him and wanted to see him?

It's all so confusing. If only they'd talked about it.

The next thing Liam knows he's not sitting quietly in Gully's garden anymore. He's up and picking lilacs. Gully was right—they're aren't many fresh blooms left. But Liam gathers what he can in his arms anyway. Because lilacs were her favourite, Gully said. Then he's heading to the cemetery with the bouquet.

Where are you, Mom? Where are you?

It's after ten o'clock. He doesn't care who's at the cemetery or what happens to him. He holds the lilacs to his face, breathing in their scent. Using them to wipe his tears.

He's tried so hard to be a good kid. For his mom. Because she worked so hard for him. Or so he's believed. And he's always planned to make her proud of him.

He was going to go to university and get a great job. He was going to earn so much money that she could do whatever she wanted. And she wouldn't need stupid Mr. Cash & Condo, because she'd have a grown up son who supported her.

But Gully sent her money every frigging month for fifteen years. She could have worked at the flower shop instead of being an escort. So why the hell did she tell him they needed the money?

He just can't get his head around that one.

He thought she hated her work! But she couldn't have hated it all that much. In fact, now he's thinking she maybe kind of liked it.

How's he supposed to deal with that?

His mom could have changed her life.

But she didn't.

Even worse, she lied to him about it.

He's at the corner of Main Street when the shadows start moving. A flickering here and there in the almost dark. First he's aware of only one kid. Then another. And another. They're surrounding him.

One of them rips the bunch of lilacs out of his arms. The purple clouds that smell like heaven go flying onto the pavement.

Just the way his mom must have when that car hit her.

What the hell's he supposed to do?

And then instead of getting the shit kicked out of him, he's running. But he's not running away from Y4C. He's running with them.

He's Ghoul Guy!

Besides Youth and Crime there's a lot of other kids—more than twenty tonight. And those dogs again. Suddenly they're moving as one being, the kids chanting, "Youth 4 Crime! Youth 4 Crime!" and the dogs barking their heads off. The kids' voices grow louder and louder until they're yelling like maniacs. "*Y4C4EVR*!"

In a flash they're taking over Main Street. Charging right down the middle, shouting and screaming.

Pulling baskets of flowers off the lampposts and hurling them everywhere.

Tearing branches off the newly planted trees that line the street. If those trees didn't have iron grills around their trunks they'd be broken right down.

Same with the garbage bins. They're made of heavy metal so they can't be tipped over. But kids can rip out the plastic liners and dump the stinking contents all over the sidewalk.

Somebody hands out bricks and baseball bats, like this is a team sport. Then they're smashing parked cars. Bashing out headlights.

Youth yells that they should trash some stores too. But most of them have bars on their windows because they've been vandalized so many times before.

The new gift shop doesn't have any yet though. It's an easy target. Kids howl with hyper glee as glass shatters and an alarm goes off. The dogs go wild. Then there's the distant sound of a police siren.

Y4C scatter. They sprint in every direction, disappearing into the darkness. It's over as fast as it began.

Back at Gully's, Liam takes a shower. But he's still high. What he did felt so bad and wrong, but so powerful. He's never had such a rush.

Something snapped in him tonight.

He crossed a line.

Maybe that's how it happened for his mom too. Maybe she didn't set out to be what she was. Maybe she just kind of got caught up in that world.

"Rampage on Main Street!" the newspaper reports the next day. There are a ton of photos of the mess Y4C made. Now Liam feels sick. He shouldn't have been part of that. What if Gully finds out?

He can't hide the paper though. Gully always reads it. "Jesus Christ!" he says when he picks it up after dinner, shaking the paper like it's to blame. "If I ever catch one of those kids!"

"Um, yeah, they really went crazy." Liam's already doing the dishes. "It says they did thousands of dollars damage." At least they didn't physically hurt anybody though. Not like that old lady. At least he didn't do something like that.

But he left that old lady lying on the sidewalk. That's just as bad. Bad as being a hit-and-run driver. No wonder he joined Y4C so easily. He's a criminal at heart. Raised by a—

"Know what I think?" Gully interrupts Liam's self torture. He turns on the TV to catch the local news. They're interviewing business owners and town councillors about the youth crime problem in Dunlane. "I think every kid in this town should spend some time in the pen. See how they like their cellmates. Let them live with lockdown. Throw them in solitary. Forget community service hours. Make them try—just for one single goddamned day—to survive inside."

"Um, yeah. I guess that might work."

Liam looks at the paper again after Gully's gone out to the garden.

Those photos make him so ashamed.

But he gets another rush just looking at them.

Circle

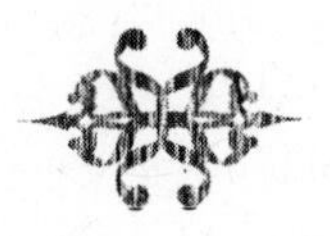

Hey Rue,

Sarita stopped by after school today. She didn't call ahead, just pulled up in our driveway. I was out in the Barley Sugar Barn helping Dad tidy up the picture frames. Usually they're stacked in a far corner and customers have to climb over some old rolled up carpets to reach them. Then they have to dig through the haphazard pile in semi-darkness to find what they want. For some reason, perhaps because his nickname is Noodle, Dad decided over the weekend to rearrange everything in the shop.

It didn't really need doing. The Barley Sugar Barn isn't an upscale antique store. It's a mishmash of bits and pieces, some in good condition, some needing a bit of paint or glue, some needing complete restoration. Customers call it charming and like to think they're going to find a deal somewhere in all that clutter. And sometimes they do. Noodle isn't in business just for the money. That would be evil capitalism. But he's really into the idea of recycling and repurposing old stuff. It makes his day if somebody buys say, an old wagon wheel he's had for years to make into a funky tabletop.

So anyway, he said he'd start the B.S. makeover with displaying the frames neatly on the walls. He asked me to help hang them up, which quite honestly felt like a make-work project for both of us. But I knew Dad was only trying to help me feel better, so I agreed to assist him. When Sarita came into the B.S. Barn, I was lifting a heavy, gilt frame that held an amateurish oil painting of a house by a mountain lake. Do you think that could be worth millions at auction? she said. I almost dropped the painting. I'd heard the car so I wasn't startled to see someone in the doorway. I was just surprised to see Sarita. She'd never come by our place before. We'd always met at her office, or talked on the phone. A creepy feeling came over me. I'd heard at school that Y4C trashed Main Street last night. Did she think I knew something about that? She helped herself to some barley sugar candy from the open jar on the counter, then came over and studied the painting I was struggling to hold. She ran her fingers along the carved acorns and ivy leaves on the frame. When she lifted her hand she had grimy dirt all over her fingers and we both laughed. I bet that frame would clean up really well, she said, brushing her hands on her jeans and nodding at the frame. How much?

You want it? It's yours, Dad said. Wow, I thought, he never makes a deal that fast. But he likes Sarita a lot. He then said, but if I were you I'd lose the painting and put a nice beveled mirror in there. The glass and window place up by the mall will cut one for you. Really? Sarita said. That would be great, but I'd have to pay you for it, I couldn't just take it. Whatever, Dad said, and we both waited. I guess he was wondering what she really wanted, too. Was this a routine checking-up-on-how-you're-all-doing visit? I've just bought an old house down by the river, she finally said. And I can't wait to furnish it with antiques, and everybody says this is the place to find what I want. Uh-huh, Dad said, that's right. The Barley Sugar Barn is where it's at.

Hey, did you buy that little wooden house by the river with the gingerbread trim and the big lot? Gardens running right back to the water? That's the one she said. Needs a lot of work but I just love it. It's so nice to be on the water, but right in town. I'll have to get an alarm system put in though, from the sound of things around Dunlane. There's so much vandalism.

I love your jeans, I said like a complete idiot, because I was worried she was going to mention what happened on Main Street, and also because I felt bad she'd had to wipe the dirt from the picture frame on them. And your haircut is fabulous too, I added. Sarita used to wear her dark hair long, but she's had it cut in a jagged bob. She has strong cheekbones and it really suits her. She gave me a counsellor look: a warm smile, which was caring but non-judgmental with kind eyes urging me to tell her everything. Mmm, that barley sugar stuff is good, she said, taking another candy, and by the way, that support group for grieving teens starts tonight. At the hospice. We've got five kids coming and we'd love to have you join us Harmony. No pressure—just come and see how you like it. You don't have to talk if you don't want to. Um, I said, I have a lot of homework, so I don't think I can make it. I almost asked her if Liam was signed up. He didn't mention it, but then, why would he? But if I thought he was going to the group I might have reconsidered. Before I could ask though, Dad looked at me and shrugged. Yeah, he likes Sarita, but he's not so keen on the group either, even if Mom thinks it's a good idea. He says most people talk about their problems too much instead of just getting on with things. I'm not sure that's very hippie of him, but hey, who am I to judge? Twenty bucks for the frame, he said. What a bargain Sarita said, paying him and taking another candy.

As she drove away Dad gave me a hug and said grieving-schmieving, group-shmoup. Then he gave me a stern parental look and added, you know anything about what happened on Main Street last night? What's the word at school?

Only that it was bad news I told him. And then to change the subject I asked if he was going to keep on with hanging up the other frames? But he said no, that's enough for today and why don't I go get busy on all that homework I have. Whew. That was close. Because everybody at school was talking about how Y4C trashed Main Street. If Dad had pushed harder I might have told him everything I know. And then I'd be beyond shunned. Plus I don't want to get Liam into trouble. I'm pretty sure he was there and helped Y4C. When I passed him in the hall at school and smiled and tried to talk to him, he pretended he didn't see me. He turned and headed the other way like he was running from a fire. He was definitely avoiding me. And why would he do that? Maybe because, like everybody else, he thinks I'm bonkers. Or maybe because he's joined Y4C and doesn't want me to know. I so hope he hasn't, but I'm so sure he probably has. And I really, really, really don't know what to do.

But then, I almost never know what to do. That's why I wander around Mount Hope & Glory Cemetery in odd clothing reading the gravestones of dead babies. Because I've no idea how to let you go and get on with my life. I'm not sure if writing this all down is helping or not. But I seem to keep doing it, so who knows, maybe it's working. I didn't buy a new journal for writing about you. Instead I chose something I found in The Barley Sugar Barn. Dad had bought a bunch of old stock from a stationery shop that was going out of business because of the big-box office supply store up at the mall. And there was a whole carton of school notebooks with quaint pictures of little kids on the front. The one I picked has a cute curly-haired girl feeding a bunny and it says "Friends." I think I liked it because I often see bunnies in the cemetery, nibbling at the grass. And also because it's kind of ironic, since I don't actually have any friends anymore. Anyway, the unlined pages are good quality, thick, not flimsy, and they're the parchment colour of the paper in some of the collectible books Mom sells. Mom says my Friends notebook is the kind of thing she used to have in elementary school and it's really called a scribbler.

It's hard to believe that kids used to write with lead pencils in books like these way back before they had calculators and computers. The multiplication tables are listed on the back cover, along with other obscure stuff I can't imagine anybody ever needing to know anymore. For instance:

Apothecaries' Weight for mixing medicines:
20 Grains = 1 Scruple

Hay and Straw Weight:
36 lb. Straw = 1 Truss, 36 Trusses = 1 Load

Imperial Dry Measure:
2 Glasses = 1 Noggin, 4 Noggins = 1 Pint

I know, I know. I'm copying all this useless information down to avoid thinking about you. But I prefer this concrete stuff to the flaky affirmations Sarita gave me to say when I'm feeling like I can't cope. Just one more, okay? Because it's my favourite:

Table of Motion: 60 Seconds = 1 Minute

60 Minutes = 1 Degree

30 Degrees = 1 Sign

12 Signs or 360 Degrees = the Circle of the earth

The circle of the earth? How profound and yet completely irrelevant is that? I love the idea of the roundness of the planet. It makes me think of a bulging pregnant belly. They don't call her Mother Earth for nothing. She's one big bump!

But I wasn't.

I started writing to you in the front of this notebook. At the back I'm copying epitaphs from the graves of the dead babies in the cemetery. Here's a few I've found so far:

Bethany Jane Smeaton, aged three days. With our Lord forever.

Percival George Chapman, aged seven months. Sleeping in Heaven.

Lucinda May Culver. Stillborn. Innocent Forever.

You'll never have a gravestone. I don't know what I'm going to do with you, but I feel certain of that. So I won't have to think of what I'd want it to say. But I need to decide soon what your final resting place will be. I can't keep carrying you around all the time. It's creepy. It's morbid. It's insane. Everybody already calls me crazy—what would they call me if they knew I take you everywhere with me? I don't want to find out.

Quickening. That's what it's called the first time a mother feels her baby move. And ohmigod it's the most incredible feeling, like there's a tiny butterfly fluttering its wings somewhere deep inside you. It happened to me the day after the ultrasound, almost as if now that I'd seen you and knew you were real I could feel you too.

I didn't feel you again for a few days and I worried like mad. But then there you were one morning in math class. It felt like you were tickling me with your toes and I almost laughed out loud. I couldn't concentrate on what the teacher was scrawling on the blackboard. Instead of writing down numbers I wrote down names I liked that started with the letters in the equations she assigned for homework:

a, b, c: Annabelle, Bethany, Camille.

x, y, z: Xanthe, Yelana, Zinnia.

I'd searched the web and found a ton of baby name sites. It was going to be hard to pick. Mom and Dad were full of suggestions and I knew they hoped I'd let them help me choose your name. Or better yet that I'd leave your naming up to them. But I had a strong feeling that somehow I'd know what to call you when I saw you. Not quite how it happened though. But I like to think your name was a gift from the universe, which is just as good.

I'd also found lots of websites that sell the most darling clothes for baby girls. I mean, it's not like I could go shopping up at the Dunlane Mall. What if somebody from school or Y4C saw me buying baby gear? And it wasn't like anybody was going to have a baby shower for me. So I spent hours looking at tiny hand-knit hats and mittens and booties, organic cotton sleepers printed with moons and stars, pretty pink flowered dresses with matching headbands and bloomers, hooded jackets with buttons shaped like fish and turtles. Oh, and shoes. The sweetest little shoes in soft multi-coloured leather appliquéd with every design you could think of. Those shoes really got to me. I couldn't decide which ones I liked best and kept changing my mind.

Mom said I didn't need to order anything right away. Since you would be a summer baby you wouldn't need a lot of clothes, just some onesies and diapers and a few receiving blankets. She said wait and get those little shoes for your baby next Christmas. Then you'll know which ones would suit her. So I waited. And now I'll never order them.

I'd also looked at maternity clothes online. My jeans and sweaters were getting way too tight and I couldn't button my shirts across my boobs. I'd soon need something else to wear. But I couldn't shop in town for new clothes either. I couldn't face other pregnant women out with their toddlers in strollers, asking me when I was due, all of them talking about their husbands and houses. And can you imagine if Christine/Crime saw me and Mom going into the maternity shop in the mall? She'd been a good enough friend to know that my parents had wanted more babies but couldn't conceive. She'd know the maternity clothes were for me. And then it would be all over town that I was pregnant. No, it would be worldwide news in minutes, because she'd post it on Facebook right away.

Anyway, I did end up getting a new look. Just not the maternity thing. Because as you know it turned out that I didn't need that kind of clothing after all. Now I wear thrift store vintage or Dazey's old prom dresses or fantasy costumes I make myself. But don't worry, I don't wear this stuff to school. I save it for going to the cemetery. I like to dress up for the dead babies.

And now I want to tell you about my favourite gravestone. It's square and grey and mossy and you can hardly read the words, but the baby buried there was called Alicia Maud McRory, the ninth child of Violet and Doran. She was born in 1877, which makes her one hundred and thirty-four years old, but she only lived five hours. I've told you that we live in the McRory House, so I'm sure there's some kind of cosmic connection between our families. Maybe someday I'll go to the library and do some research and find out more. But for now I just like to sit by Alicia Maud's grave and meditate and try to connect with your soul, wherever it is. I try to make sense of what happened. There's a little angel, which I think is called a cherub, perched on top of the McRory family's gravestone, like it's guarding her. I love that little stone cherub. I feel like it's somehow watching over you too.

In

Around school, some Y4Cs start making eye contact with Liam. A few kids he'd pick out as 4s right away. Army surplus clothes, boots and chains, piercings, tattoos and shaved heads or look-at-me hair. Others he never would have guessed if he hadn't seen them in action on Main Street. They're more the good student with a great future type. Like Liam.

One thing his mom always insisted on—that he dress well. And she didn't mean hip or trendy. She meant dress to impress teachers and bosses. She meant dress respectably, so nobody will ask too many questions.

None of the 4s actually speak to Liam. But a couple nod, and they all look at him different. Like he's proved himself. Like he's okay. For the first time in his life, he belongs.

He's a 4!

He's Ghoul Guy!

He's *in*!

He's never been part of anything before.

Didn't play team sports. Didn't go to Boy Scouts or summer camp. Didn't hang with any of the social groups at his old school.

Sure, he said he'd never join Y4C. And he didn't really mean to. It just kind of happened. But man, it feels good. Scary but cool.

The principal makes a special announcement saying how upset Dunlane District High School is over the vandalism on Main Street. Saying that anyone knowing anything about what happened should come forward. Promising that all names will be kept confidential. Just please tell a parent, a teacher, or the police.

Yeah, right. Of course nobody does. Y4C might trash stuff, but they'd never rat. And anybody else would be way too afraid of them to say anything.

Liam sees the strange girl he met in the cemetery around school too. Harmony appears out of nowhere, startling him more than once. His heart races. She is so gorgeous! And in jeans she looks perfectly normal. But she stares at him with her head tilted to one side, her eyebrows raised like she wants an explanation. Which makes things awkward.

Since they met he's been thinking about her non-stop, wanting to get to know her. He'd like to smile and say hey. But she won't want to be friends if she finds out he was down on Main Street on Saturday night. Once she knows he's a 4, she'll hate him.

So he tries to avoid her.

But she won't let him get away with that. On Wednesday she comes by his locker. She doesn't speak, just stands there blocking his way. He can't escape. Not that he wants to. Her soft grey T-shirt makes him think of baby birds. Or kittens. He grips his textbooks to keep from touching her.

Then she leans right in toward him, her shimmery hair brushing his face. She smells sweet and herbal, like Gully's garden after a rain. "Saturday morning," she breathes into his ear. "The cemetery. See you there."

Thursday and Friday take forever to pass. Liam goes to classes but can't focus on schoolwork. When he's sitting at his desk, one or the other of his legs keeps jittering.

At home he waters the tomato plants for something to do. He soaks the soil but doesn't get the leaves wet, just as Gully's taught him. That calms him a bit, but not enough. He's still jumpy.

If only he could go swimming, burn off some stress. He doesn't miss Mr. Cash & Condo, but he sure misses the pool in his building. He longs for the gapped out feeling he used to get after doing laps for an hour.

Gully's on night shift so there's no one to talk to. Liam's alone, obsessing about being a 4.

His mom would kill him.

But she's the one who's dead.

If she hadn't gone out that night, he'd never have had to come live here in DumpLane. He'd never have met Youth and Crime. He'd never have heard of Y4C.

So who's really to blame?

Saturday morning Liam picks some flowers for his mom and sets out for the cemetery. Now that he's a 4 he can go wherever he wants. Whenever he wants.

His only fear is that he'll end up telling Harmony what he did. Because what if she asks him directly? He doesn't want to lie to her. And then he'd have to tell her all about his mom. Why he was mad enough that night to join Y4C and trash Main Street.

And would Harmony accept that excuse? She might still blame him for getting involved. For not resisting Y4C's influence. For not doing the right thing and running away from them.

Harmony's waiting for him at the cemetery, sitting on his mom's grave. Today she's dressed all in shades of white. She seems to be wearing layers of skirts and tops with lots of lace and beads. Her outfit looks like it might be made from old tablecloths or maybe wedding dresses. On her head sits a ring of leaves and flowers.

She looks stunning, like some kind of fantasy figure. Liam can barely breathe. He can't even speak. He just stands there in awe.

"Hey," she says, "Nice tulips."

He puts the bouquet down by the gravestone. "My grandfather grew them." He's glad to see that someone has cleared away the dead funeral flower arrangements. All that's left are last week's lilacs. He carries those over to the cemetery compost bin by the outdoor tap. Fills the green plastic watering can the caretaker keeps there. Lugs it back to his mom's grave. Tries to soak the still non-sprouting grass seed.

"Watering it like that's not going to help much," Harmony says. "Don't they have a hose or a sprinkler?"

"We're not supposed to use that much water." Pete the caretaker was very specific on water conservation. "But my grandfather says he'll plant some more seed in the fall when it's rainy. He says by next summer this will be all flat and green, like the rest of the cemetery. Well, like the rest of the new part."

Being there with Harmony makes Liam blab on like an idiot. He wants to talk and talk and talk to her. About anything. And everything. Except Y4C. But as he feared, that's all she wants to discuss.

"So Y4C really destroyed Main Street last week," she says, giving him that same questioning look she did at school. Like she's waiting for a confession. Well, let her wait.

"Yeah, I heard about that. Nasty!" He goes and hauls more water.

"You know what?" Harmony says when he comes back. She moves over so he can soak the grass seed where she was sitting. "You're not going to believe this, but I used to hang with them last year."

He almost drops the watering can. "You did?" But she's so spacey and gentle. He can't picture Harmony vandalizing anything. "You were a 4?"

"No, no. I was never an actual 4. It was before they were called that." She tucks her bare feet up under her ruffly skirts. "At first it was kind of a thrill, you know?"

Oh, yeah. He knows. But he's sure not going to admit it.

"And I was, like, totally in love with Youth."

"In love with Youth?" No. Oh please, no. He so doesn't want to believe her. But he can tell by the way her face flushes that it's true. "So what happened?"

She wrinkles up her nose like something smells bad. "Remember that Halloween party thing I told you about? When the cemetery got trashed?"

"Sure, I've heard about it around school." He tries to be funny, saying in a spooky voice, "The Legend of the Lost Tombstones, ooooohhh!" And then, in a truly scared voice, "You were part of that?"

"Yeah, well, like I said, it was before they were called Y4C. And Youth was still called Jordan." She untucks her feet and stretches out her legs, fluffing the fabric of her skirt over them. Today she has her toenails painted indigo, with little silver moon and star decals on top. "Some bad stuff happened. Really, really bad stuff. And then Jordan changed his name to Youth and started calling his gang Youth 4 Crime, and he hooked up with this girl called Christine, who used to be my best friend before she changed her name to Crime, and they decided that everybody had to get a stupid tattoo to show they're a 4 and oh who cares anyway? They think they're so edgy, but they're all such losers."

Jordan? So that's his real name. And Crime used to be Harmony's best friend? He'd like to know more about that. But first he asks, "What tattoo?"

"It's supposed to be a gang member thing. Like any of them would ever survive in a real gang."

He doesn't want to get inked. And don't you have to be like, sixteen or eighteen or something? There's no way Gully would sign for him. "What's it look like?"

"*Y4C4EVR!*"

Of course. He saw it on Youth that first day at his locker. He laughs out loud because it's so predictable. "How stupid is that?" But what if they make him use a fake ID? What if they make him go to a place where they don't ask too many questions? Would he be able to hide a tattoo from Harmony? Or from Gully?

He carries the watering can back to the tap. His mom had a butterfly tattoo on her shoulder. And a yin yang sign on her ankle. And a rosebud somewhere he didn't want to see. She got that one when she met Mr. Cash & Condo.

She called it body art, and said it represented her life blossoming. She said it signified hope for a future full of flowers. He's pretty sure she didn't mean her son bringing flowers to her grave.

He goes back and sits down beside Harmony. So what if he gets wet from the ground where he watered the grass seed. He just wants to be close to her.

"So," she says, "you were going to tell me about your mom?"

Since she asked him last time, he's been thinking what to say. He's ready with a rehearsed story. "Oh, my mom was great. She was really young when she had me, so we were more like friends than parent and kid. We did a lot of fun stuff together. Like, this one time, she rented a BMW and took me to the zoo. And she always baked me a special chocolate fudge birthday cake. And we had a great condo. She kept it really nice." All true so far.

"What was her job?"

The dreaded question. "She worked in a flower shop called Sprigs & Twigs at the corner of our street." A complete lie. But possible. That's what his mom always said she wanted to do. When she gave up the game. She said that if Mr. Cash & Condo ever came through on his promises, she'd go learn floral design.

She hoped they'd hire her at Sprigs & Twigs, because she'd given them so much business over the years. That's probably what her rose tattoo really symbolized—her plans for a whole new life with a respectable job. But all he tells Harmony is, "My mom was really good at arranging flowers. My grandfather loves to garden. I guess that's where she learned it."

"And your dad?"

Ah, the next dreaded question. His dad was a sperm donor, his mom always said. And that's all she'd say. Liam figures his dad was a one-night stand. Or maybe she didn't even know who he was. "No idea." And he's never spent a lot of time wondering about his dad either. It was clear the guy didn't care about them. So why should Liam care about him? "It was just me and my Mom."

Harmony tucks her feet up under her skirt again. She wraps her arms around herself, as if she's cold. "And I heard she was killed in a car accident?" Her voice goes all sad and sorry. Oh Christ, please don't let him start to cry. He's not sure he can talk about this.

"Yeah. A hit-and-run." His voice breaks like he's twelve years old. But then he looks at Harmony's strange dress and the weird wreath in her hair. She's obviously someone who has suffered too. She might not understand him being a 4. But he guesses she just might understand grief. He goes on. "It might have been a drunk driver or somebody street racing. They're still investigating."

"I am so, so sorry," she says. "I mean, I didn't know her or anything, but still, to die like that, it's just not fair."

"Yeah, it never should have happened."

And then something truly incredible happens.

Kiss

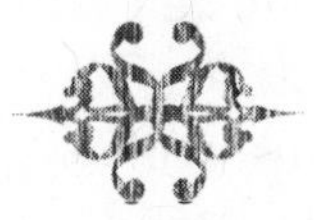

Harmony opens her arms to Liam. "That's so brutal about your Mom." Her embrace is full of understanding. "How awful for you." She means what he just told her about his mom getting killed in an accident. She's still got no idea about her being an escort, about Arabella Investments and Mr. Cash & Condo and all that.

He's sorry he had to make up that story about his mom working for a florist. But he couldn't risk scaring Harmony away. He wants to sit here on his mom's grave with this amazing girl in her frothy fairytale dress forever.

"Yeah," he says. "It's been tough." But being hugged by Harmony feels so good. Her hair smells like vanilla today and he can't help reaching up to stroke it. When he does though, the wreath of leaves and flowers she's wearing falls off. "Oops, sorry!" He tries to put the silly thing back on her head. But it keeps slipping off her shiny hair.

"Never mind." She places the wreath on Liam's head instead. Then the whole thing falls apart and they both laugh. Harmony gathers up all the stems and places them beside the white tulips Liam brought. "At least you have your grandfather." Her voice sounds like her hair feels in his hands. Soft and silky. "That's something."

"Yeah, Gully's okay." He knows it's not every guy who would come through like that for a grandkid he didn't even know. "He's done his best for me since the accident. And I'm really glad I've gotten to know him. But I'd still rather have my mom alive."

Harmony hugs him again.

He leans into her arms and asks, "Do you ever wish you could go back and change something you did?"

"Yeah, all the time." Harmony's arms drop from his shoulders and the hug ends. "Every freaking day."

He waits, but she doesn't explain. So he says, "My mom asked if I minded her going on a date that night she got killed. And yeah, I did mind. I was really pissed off. We were supposed to be going to a movie together. But then this guy she liked called her, well, this guy she was thinking of getting married to."

"And you told her it was okay? That she should go have fun?"

"Exactly. So the last thing I said to my mom was nice and supportive. And I will *always* regret that. Because if I'd told her how mad I really was, she probably wouldn't have gone. She was big on not breaking plans with me."

Harmony smoothes at her lacy sleeves, like she's checking out the stitching. Maybe she made the dress herself. It kind of looks like it. Or maybe she borrowed it from a museum or a theatre or something. She makes a sighing sound, like she's close to tears. "I'm sure you miss her a lot."

"Yeah," he says. "Yeah, I do." Why'd he have to go and be all mature that night? Why'd he say, whatever, they'd go to a movie another time? Christ, he feels rotten about that. "I guess I should be glad that the last thing I said to her was nice, but if I could, I'd take it back. I'd say something mean and sarcastic and then she might still be alive."

"You can't know that for sure." Harmony straightens her back against the gravestone and folds her hands in her lap.

"Maybe it was just her time to go, like even though she was so young and all."

"You really believe in fate?"

"I don't know." She shrugs. "Sometimes I do. Sometimes I don't."

Again he waits for her to go on. Because he can tell she's thought a lot about this. But she doesn't. So finally he says, "You know what? Let's talk about something else."

Harmony pats his back, then smiles and reaches into her patchwork shoulder bag. "I've got something to show you," she says, taking out a notebook. It's old-fashioned looking, made of faded newsprint. And it has a cutesy picture of a little girl feeding a rabbit on the front.

"Where'd you get that? An antique store?"

"Actually, I did." She opens it to the back page. "Ever hear of The Barley Sugar Barn?"

"The what?"

"The Barley Sugar Barn. It's on Fergus Street. Behind the McRory house? You can't live in Dunlane and not have noticed it. Even if you're new here."

He has to stop and think. It's not like he's been paying a lot of attention to stuff like that. "I guess I've maybe seen it. I walk down that street all the time."

"Well, we live in the McRory House. And my Dad has his business—antiques and collectibles—out in the barn. But never mind that." She opens her notebook. "Listen to these epitaphs from the gravestones of my dead babies."

And then she starts reading aloud in a dramatic voice:

> *"Matilda Hope Hallowell, aged 1 year, 7 days, with the Angels in Glory. Hector Everett Trow, beloved son of —"*

"Hey!" He grabs the notebook from her. "Stop it! That's so gruesome!"

"Not to me," she says. "I've recorded seventeen so far." She grabs her notebook back and tucks it away. "Those babies are the only friends I have now."

"You have me." And then they're hugging again. Right on his mom's grave. Harmony is holding him tight and he's tangling his fingers in her hair. Their lips meet. Hers are soft, like flower petals.

Maybe his life might not be so bad after all. But then all of a sudden Harmony pulls away. "Okay," she says. "Cool it." She jumps up and adjusts her dress, pulls a white ribbon out of her bag and ties back her hair. "I have to go."

He's kind of disoriented. "Why?" He looks all around, wondering what just happened. His body wants her back. "Is there somebody here? Some 4s or something?"

"No, no, don't worry," she says. "It's not that. It's just, um, I have to be home right now." Then she runs—not walks—away from him.

He watches her disappear. Was he that klutzy? Okay, he wrecked her leafy crown thing, but she didn't seem to mind. She laughed about it. And she didn't leave then. She stayed with him. She listened to him. And when she kissed him, it sure felt good. She was as into it as he was.

So what went wrong?

He's still wondering when he sees see Youth and Crime. Where'd they come from? They weren't there when Harmony left. But now they're sitting on one of the memorial benches nearby, smoking.

He doesn't move. He waits while they come to him.

Youth's wearing a black bandana over his ratty hair. He's tied it so that the white skull printed on it sits smack in the middle of his forehead. Profound. "Hey, Ghoul Guy," he says. "Whatcha doing?"

"What's it look like?"

"Looks like you were trying to have sex on your mommy's grave with my old friend Harm. But you didn't get no satisfaction, right?"

No need to answer that.

"Bad move, hanging with Harm," Crime says. Her ragged jeans are so low and tight he doesn't know how she can wear them. "That chick's crazy. She's like, totally out of her mind."

"What I was doing," Liam says, "is none of your business."

Youth stubs out his cigarette on the Hall family's gravestone. He makes sure to grind some ashes into Liam's Mom's name. "Mommy's boy brought her some flowers, I see." He picks up the white tulips.

Crime steps closer and rubs herself against Liam. She's wearing a skanky black top that laces up the front and shows a lot of skin. "Hey, how come you never bring me flowers, Ghoul Guy?" Her voice is sexy, like she thinks he's hot. She grabs his crotch and laughs. "Thought so," she says. "Hard for Harm? Or maybe for me?" She turns and flashes the tattoo on her lower back. *Y4C4EVR!* "I know you want me," she says.

Youth whistles. "Or maybe you want them both together? Harm and Crime. What a combo." He shreds tulip petals all over Liam's Mom's grave. "Grass is never gonna grow here, you know, if you keep fooling around like that on it."

"Shame, shame," Crime says. "What would your mommy say? If she could still talk, that is."

Liam laughs. To stop himself from killing them both. And because they've no idea that it's a trick question.

Thing is, his mom wouldn't be upset.

She was always after him to find a girlfriend. She didn't seem to get that he couldn't and wouldn't, not with her running Arabella Investments. She always acted like that shouldn't be an issue. So she'd be glad he's met somebody. She'd like Harmony.

And she wouldn't give a hoot about where they were fooling around.

All he'd get from his mom would be a lecture on safe sex and condoms.

"Ya did good down on Main Street." Youth throws the wrecked tulip stems down on top of the shredded petals and the remains of Harmony's crown.

"Yeah," Crime says. "We're impressed."

And then they strut away, tipping over containers of flowers on other graves as they go.

"Party tonight, Ghoul Guy," Youth calls back to Liam. "Be here."

Friends

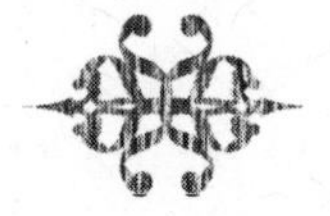

Hey Rue,

Ohmigod, ohmigod, ohmigod! I've touched him. I've hugged him. I've even kissed him! A lot! Here's what happened. I got tired of Liam avoiding me at school so I went up to him at his locker and demanded that he meet me at the cemetery on Saturday morning. I didn't give him a chance to say no. In fact he didn't say anything at all, just stood there looking stunned as I walked away. So then today, for meeting him, I wore this dress I sewed from three old wedding dresses I found at the thrift store. I can't believe anyone would give away her wedding dress, but I guess if you'd already bought it and then the wedding was cancelled, or you got divorced or something, you might not want it anymore. One of them I'm sure was never even worn.

Anyway, I used the flowing skirt of one, the beaded bodice of another, and the lacy sleeves of another. I basted it by hand first, because the fabric was really slippery, and pins weren't enough to keep it from sliding. And I also wanted to make sure the pieces all looked good together before I sewed it on the machine. I had to make a few adjustments to get the fit just right, but in the end I was pysched with my creation. The dress makes me look like a goddess.

And I have to tell you about my toenails. They look cosmic! Last night I painted them a dark, midnight blue and stuck on silver moon and star decals. And then I washed my hair and braided it while it was still wet, and when I brushed it out this morning it was all shiny and wavy. I'd sewn a beaded hair band cut from one of the wedding dresses, but decided in the morning to make something even prettier. So I wove some strands of ivy and pink rosebuds from the garden together into a wreath and pinned that on top of my head. Then I went to the cemetery.

You might think my parents would wonder at me heading out wearing flowers in my hair and a refashioned wedding gown. But I've always liked to dress up in costumes, ever since I was three years old. There's something about pretending to be someone else that makes me happy. Not that I'm happy these days, but it makes me feel better. That's why I was so into wearing my purple velvet, medieval princess dress to that Halloween cemetery party. Because I wanted to be that princess. So this morning, it wasn't like my parents had never seen me in strange clothes. And it wasn't like my dress actually looked like a traditional wedding dress. It was more of a fantasy gown.

But in the end Mom and Dad didn't notice me leaving the house at all. Because it's Saturday, The Barley Sugar Barn was open and Noodle was out there waiting for customers. Dazey was in her office, most likely checking her eBay accounts. Or wrapping up packages for shipping. She didn't used to work on weekends, but now she does. She's always in her office these days. I guess that's how she deals with you being gone. Or else she's into one of those role-playing games or something. Or she's having an online affair. So I left a note on the kitchen table that said: Walking. Home for lunch.

You might also think that I wouldn't wander through town decked out like I was an extra in a movie or something. But I don't care if I get laughed at. If kids don't like me the way I am, too bad. If they diss me and post stuff online, who cares? Nothing will change what happened. Nothing will bring you back. That's not to say I'm not careful when I go out. I don't want to get beaten up. I only dress fancy for visiting the cemetery, and I only go there early on Saturday mornings, before Youth or Crime or any 45 are about. I'd never dream of wearing such an outfit to school. There, I try to blend in. No, actually, at school I try to be invisible. But anyway, back to this morning.

First I visited the graves of all the dead babies I've found so far. I didn't take the time to search for more like I usually do because I didn't want to miss seeing Liam. I went straight to the new part of the cemetery and waited at his mother's grave. She has this pink granite gravestone, all carved with birds and flowers, that she shares with his grandmother. According to the dates, she was only thirty-two years old when she died. I wonder what it was like for him, having such a young mother? She was probably way more fun than my Mom, who is practically a senior citizen. I mean, Mom was over forty when she had me. And even with her dark hair and great legs, she's been mistaken for my grandmother more than once. Which really upsets her. But whatever.

I was still thinking about Liam's mother when he showed up, carrying a bouquet of white tulips. He is so nice to bring fresh flowers to his mom. And I could tell by his face that he thought I looked fabulous. Well, interesting, at least. He did a double take on my hair wreath, then he kind of smiled and stared at my bare feet. I willed the little silver moon and star decals on my toes to cast an enchanting spell on him. We talked for a bit while he watered the new grass seed on the grave. Then I got up my nerve and told him about the Halloween party in the cemetery, and how I used to like Youth, back when he was still just called Jordan.

What a relief. I was so worried about how Liam would react, but he didn't seem too shocked. He was actually more interested in the Y4C tattoo, almost like he wanted to get one or something, which confirms what I've suspected, that he's a 4 now. But I didn't ask him about that. I guess I'm afraid of the answer.

Then I showed him my Friends notebook. Not the front part where I write this stuff to you, but the back pages where I've listed all the dead babies. I started to read some of their names and epitaphs, because I love how they sound. But he sure didn't want to hear that. He acted like he thought that was really twisted. And okay, it is, I know it is. But I can't stop writing them down. Liam didn't leave then though. So he couldn't have been that creeped out. He stayed there with me and told me about his mother and how she died.

I pretended I didn't know any of it, but I already knew the basic story from listening to my parents talk at dinner. Dad gets all the local gossip at The Barley Sugar Barn. On Mondays he's closed but people make appointments to bring in things that he might want to buy—furniture, china, paintings—whatever they have kicking around in their basement or attic. It's mostly older folks who come in then, wanting to downsize, get rid of a lifetime of clutter. And they all eat some barley sugar candy while he listens to them talk about the old days and what's going on in town. So of course he'd heard all about Gully Hall's grandson coming to live with him and why. He said there was some other talk about Liam's mother, but it didn't bear repeating. I couldn't help but remember that picture of her I saw in the newspaper with her obituary when she died, the one showing her as Miss Dunlane 1996. I wonder what the rumours Dad won't talk about are? What's the real story? And I wonder if Liam will ever trust and like me enough to tell me?

See, I got the feeling he was hiding something about his mother. He said she worked in a flower shop, but then he acted really tense and phony when he was talking about it, like maybe she got fired or something. But who could get fired from a flower shop? And he said he didn't care who his father was, but I know that can't be true. He was way too casual about it. Every kid cares about stuff like that. Maybe they won't always admit it, but they care.

Anyway, then the kissing thing just kind of happened. It started out that Liam stroked my hair and then he got it all tangled up in his fingers and then my wreath fell off and we laughed a lot. He tried to put the wreath back on my head but it fell apart and then we kissed. Like really, really kissed for a long time. And then I had a flashback to kissing Jordan that horrible Halloween night and what happened in the caretaker's office. And then I got so confused about everything, how sorry I am that I ever kissed Jordan and how much I hate him now, and how good it felt kissing Liam and how much I really like him. So there was nothing to do but stop. I was sorry to do that to him, I mean leave him there all hot and bothered, but sometimes you just have to save yourself. So I did. I stood up and ran away from him.

Rush

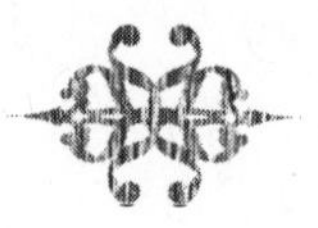

Liam hides in his room for the whole afternoon. Gully wants him to help in the garden, but Liam can't face that. The memory of trashing Main Street with Y4C is too strong. He can't risk getting all buddy-buddy with Gully and confessing over the tomatoes. So he says he needs to study for exams. Which is true. He does need to study. It's just not what he's doing today.

What he's doing is reliving his morning in the cemetery with Harmony. Obsessing about her flowing hair and lovely face. Wondering how insane she might be. Would someone in her right mind record the names and stuff on dead babies' graves? Then he's daydreaming about her sweet kisses. How great her body felt against his. And so on. Their encounter replays in his head and groin, over and over and over, for hours.

But even thoughts of Harmony can't keep Youth and Crime from sneaking into his mind. That tattoo on Crime's lower back: *Y4C4EVR!* That party in the cemetery tonight. Will he go?

He knows he shouldn't. His mom would be so disappointed in him.

Besides violence, she really hated any kind of vandalism. She used to stop people in the street and tell them to pick up their litter. And most of them did what she said. Maybe they were embarrassed to be scolded or maybe they were knocked out by her beauty. But they never told her to f-off or anything.

They picked up whatever they'd dropped, coffee cups, sandwich wrappers, even cigarette butts, and dumped them in the nearest garbage bin.

But even though his mom would freak, a little part of Liam can't wait to go to the cemetery tonight. Just to feel alive. He's been numb since she died. Except for that night on Main Street. And then today, with Harmony, when he really started to feel something again. Both in his heart and his body.

He wants more of that. More, more, more.

But there's Gully to consider too. He clipped the article from the paper about the vandalism on Main Street and left it lying on the kitchen table for a couple days. Then it turned up on Liam's desk. Probably Gully hopes he'll be a good kid and tell him who did it. Or confess to something.

Like that's ever going to happen. Looking at those pictures just makes Liam want to do more damage. He doesn't feel guilty. He feels excited. It's almost as good as fantasizing about Harmony.

So what should he do about the party? For sure his mom would tell him to forget it. She'd say you're a big boy now and free to make your own choices. *Make the right ones*. Which is pretty much exactly what Gully would say too.

But his mom is dead. She went and got herself killed. When they didn't even need the money. What was she thinking? And look at the choices she made.

Her working name was *Kandi*, for god's sake. And *Kandi* was proud of her high rating on an obscene website that ranks escorts. He can't see how running an escort service disguised as an investment company was a better choice for his mom's whole life than him going to one party for one night.

And as for Gully, he's on evening shift this week. He won't be around to ask questions. So after Gully leaves for work, Liam heads for the party.

He knows it's stupid. But there's nothing else to do in DumpLane. He's starved for belonging. And hungry for the rush.

At night the cemetery gates are closed. The caretaker, Gully's friend Pete, comes by at dusk to lock them. But that only keeps vehicles out. Kids can climb over the fence. They know the cops are busy elsewhere. So there's nobody and nothing to stop them.

Things are in full swing when Liam shows up. There's a lot more kids than he's seen with Y4C before. A huge mob is partying in the new part of the cemetery. Way too close his mom's grave.

Almost on his mom's grave.

Tonight the dogs are off leash, snuffling around at the pop cans and beer bottles and fast food garbage all over the ground. He tries not to think about how angry all that litter would make his mom.

It makes Liam mad too, but he's too chicken to do anything about it. Something tells him he wouldn't get the reaction his mom used to. Nobody in Y4C is going to say, oh sorry man, and go pick it all up. He'd more likely get head butted or punched in the gut.

Loud music throbs. Kids are lying on sleeping bags under the trees, smoking up. Somebody hands Liam a beer and he chugs it down. He doesn't like the taste. But he likes the feeling.

He takes another. Makes sure Youth and Crime see him drinking, because he wants points for being here. And for joining in. Then he wanders around trying to be invisible. He also needs to stay in control.

Kids are talking about grave robbers in the old days. How they'd dig up dead bodies to steal their jewellery or gold fillings from their teeth. Then they're all excited about the hot market right now for stuff stolen from cemeteries. Some antique dealers will pay for old stone statues and urns and crosses. They can sell them to rich people for their private gardens. Some scrap metal dealers will pay for the bronze plaques from memorial trees and benches and even the markers where ashes are buried.

But not the guy at The Barley Sugar Barn, they say. Don't go there, man. He's an old pothead but he's straight. He'd call the cops. They must be talking about Harmony's father. Liam knows better than to let on that he knows her. That he's talked to her. That he's kissed her.

But then kids start talking about sex. Somebody says it would be cool to do it in a coffin. Or at least on a grave.

"Why don't you ask Ghoul Guy about that?" It's Youth's voice, right behind Liam. Didn't even know he was there. "We saw him with Harm this morning. They were doing it on his mommy's grave."

Everybody laughs.

"Tell us all about it." Crime comes at him out of the darkness. "I've heard the Ice Queen Supreme is easy."

"Oh yeah?" It's a huge effort to stop himself from reacting with violence. But starting a fight won't help Harmony. "Where'd you hear that?"

Crime drains her beer can, chucks it at a gravestone. A dog snarls and goes chasing after it. "Youth. And everybody else. You shoulda seen her last Halloween." She holds up her cellphone. "Wanna check the pictures out?"

He'd like to beat both Youth and Crime to a bloody pulp. God, they're sick. They'd probably shut up if he went along with them and pretended that he and Harmony really did it.

But he can't treat Harmony like that. He remembers how great holding her and kissing her felt. "You know what?" He chugs down some more beer. "Sex in a cemetery is way overrated."

Everybody hoots and guffaws. Like that's the funniest thing anybody's ever said. But then, they're all either drunk or high.

"When you getting your ink?" Youth says. "Better be soon."

"Sure, sure." Not a chance. What's he trying to prove here anyway? Okay, so he's never been invited to a party before. But he's not that desperate.

Yes, he is.

He's so frigging lonely. He's been lonely all his life. He never had any friends because of his mom. And since she was hardly ever home at night, he watched too much TV. He played too many video games. All by himself. And even when she was home after school, she was busy. Then she was getting ready for work. Doing her hair and makeup. Putting on her short tight dress. Stepping into her high heels.

"Okay 4s," Youth shouts. "Let's go!" He forces a can of spray paint into Liam's hand. "*Y4C4EVR!*" he yells. "Tag mommy's gravestone. Now."

What? Youth wants him to prove himself by putting up graffiti on his mom's gravestone? He can't do that. It would be so wrong. And she hated graffiti. She didn't find it cool and artistic. She said it showed a lack of respect.

But Y4C is waiting.

If he doesn't do it, what will they do to him?

He stalls. Pretends to drink more beer. Maybe he can distract them. "Nah, too boring." He tosses his empty beer can like Crime did, dinging his mom's gravestone. "See that bench over there? Let's burn it!"

They all follow as Ghoul Guy runs toward the bench. He can feel the rush rising inside him. The rush that pushes away his last bit of self-control. The rush that lets his rage about his mom and her death consume him.

The rush that's worth any risk.

"Gimme a lighter," he yells as he leads them on. Youth tosses him one and he flicks it open. Holds the flame to the wood. Tries not to see the bronze plaque on the back of the bench that reads: *In Loving Memory of ...*

The bench doesn't catch fire right away. A lot of kids attack it with lighters, but it just blackens and smokes. The dogs go insane.

Then Crime sets a dried-up bouquet on fire. She twirls it around in the air like a sparkler. When she can't hold it anymore she flings it onto the bench.

Then they're all grabbing flower baskets and dead grass and garbage—anything that will burn. They're making a bonfire. On somebody's memorial bench. *In Loving Memory of ...*

With a whoosh it finally goes up in flames.

Y4C dance around it shrieking like devils. Then there's the sound of sirens. Cops? Fire trucks?

Who the hell cares?

They can't be caught.

Y4C4EVR!

Blood

Hey Rue,

Sarita called again today, not that I talked to her. But I can easily guess what she wanted. And it wasn't antique furniture from the Barley Sugar Barn. She's already been back a couple times to look around, supposedly for stuff for her house, but conveniently coming by when she knows I'll be home from school. Both times I saw her car pull up though and hid in the house to avoid her. And since that day when she bought the picture frame, she's left me lots of light and breezy messages: Hi Harmony, how's it going? Just letting you know there's still space in that teen grief group, give me a call back sometime, okay?

Yeah, right. Like that's ever going to happen.

Mom did talk to her though. Because I'll never pick up the phone when she calls, Mom uses the time for her own personal therapy. She loves talking to Sarita. Honestly, sometimes I think my parents need more help than I do. Noodle because he won't talk about you at all. I mean, I know I don't talk about you either, but at least I'm writing about you. Somehow I don't think he's keeping a bereavement journal to soothe his soul. And Dazey, ohmigod, she never stops talking about you. Ever. Her phone conversation with Sarita today, the part I could overhear, which wasn't hard because her voice gets so loud when she's worked up, was all about our huge loss and how devastated she still is. She cried and cried and carried on for ages.

I asked Mom after she hung up if it's normal for a counsellor to have so much time on her hands? Doesn't Sarita have a life? Maybe she likes you and maybe she considers grief a serious issue, Mom said, and of course I couldn't answer back on that one. Or maybe Sarita's one in a million, Mom went on, at least that's my impression of her, and why don't you call her, it couldn't hurt, could it?

Well yeah Mom, actually, it could. Hurt. A lot. A whole hell of a lot. It hurts every single second of every single day and talking to Sarita the exceptional counsellor won't really change that. Oh sure, I might feel better for an hour or two afterwards, but then when I wake up in the middle of the night I'll feel worse. Way worse. Because even if I called Sarita then, and I know I could call her anytime at all, but even if I did call her at three a.m., you, my dear little Rue, will still be gone.

Remember when I told you about quickening? How cool it was to feel you alive and moving? Well, the day after I felt you fluttering about inside me in math class, I started bleeding. Just spotting at first, which Dr. Wembley said when Mom phoned could be nothing to worry about, but then I got the worst cramps and lower back pain I'd ever had and the bleeding got heavier and then blood just started gushing out of me like a river. Honestly. I have never, ever, ever, seen so much blood! Luckily it happened after I came home from school because I couldn't stop the flow with pads or towels or anything and I started feeling like I might pass out so Mom rushed me to the hospital. And after that everything is kind of blurry but Mom says I bled and bled and then they did another ultrasound and said they'd lost your heartbeat and that I was having a miscarriage. Of course we both went nuts and then Dad came and tried to calm Mom and me down. The nurses did their best to settle us too. They told us that a miscarriage is a natural event that happens for a medical reason. It can't be stopped and it wasn't my fault. Not at all. They gave me a ton of painkillers but it was all still so awful. I was groggy and scared and devastated. And then after hours and hours of labour you were born. Dead. And after that I still had to have a D&C to make sure that every last shred of fetal tissue came out. And finally after that they said I was "complete." What an insult! Because of course I was just the opposite.

They said you were fully formed and they couldn't see anything obvious wrong with you. Well, nothing except that your heart wasn't beating and you weren't breathing, which seems pretty obvious to me. You were dead. That's what was wrong with you. And nobody could tell me why. They all kept blabbing on, trying to comfort me with facts such as that fifteen to twenty percent of pregnancies end in miscarriage and there was nothing anyone could have done to save you. And I shouldn't worry because being so young I still had years and years ahead of me to have fine, healthy babies. Mom freaked over that one, but that was more about her than me, because of her not being able to get pregnant later in life when she was emotionally and financially ready for babies.

And then I asked what would happen to you and they told me again not to worry, they would look after everything. What is everything? I wanted to know. At first they didn't want to tell me, but Mom and Dad insisted. So they told us that according to medical guidelines, a fetus is not a person until twenty weeks gestation. If you had been over twenty weeks old when you died you would be called a stillbirth. But since you were only nineteen weeks, and smaller than a pound of butter, you were considered "miscarried fetal tissue" and no death certificate could be issued. Oh, and you couldn't be buried. You were stuck in the shadows forever. The grey area, they called it. And so even though you already had a face and fingerprints and could yawn and stretch and suck they would dispose of you as medical waste.

I should have been hysterical but I was so doped up I just said oh. That's it. Oh. And then I sobbed and wept and I couldn't stop because I didn't want them to just toss you into the pathology department's garbage and incinerate you along with all the tumors and diseased organs and amputated body parts. But I was too traumatized to stand up for you.

Luckily Mom and Dad took charge and asserted our rights and made sure you got more humane treatment. Mom used her best British accent and Dad was diplomatic and persistent. They were exhausted and just wanted to go home and cry, but they insisted on discussing other options. And they demanded to see you. After a lot of back and forth with the staff on duty, a nurse finally gave in and brought what she called your "remains" in a tiny basket lined with a scrap of blanket. I couldn't look. Mom and Dad tried to convince me I should, they said I'd regret it later if I didn't meet you and say goodbye. But I just couldn't. If I had to let you go forever it was better this way.

I want you to know though that it wasn't because I didn't care about you that I couldn't look. Please believe me, Rue. It was because I cared too much. I hope that makes some sense and you can forgive me for not wanting to see you. And I'm sure you remember Mom and Dad talking to you about how they wanted to be your grandparents more than anything, and about the nursery they'd been preparing, and the quilt Mom was making, and the cradle Dad was refinishing, and what a good mother I would have been to you. And I would have. I hope you know that. If you had lived I promise I would have devoted my life to you. My whole entire life.

It was while Mom and Dad were talking to you that Sarita the grief counsellor showed up for the first time. I guess one of the nurses called her in, because of Mom and Dad making such a fuss about humane treatment for you. And Sarita was so nice and understanding that I cried even more. She tactfully discussed the issue of you being a real person to us, but not necessarily in the eyes of the world. She said it has a lot to do with the laws about abortion. Because if you were considered a person at nineteen weeks, then how could abortions be allowed up to twenty weeks? And that made things so extremely difficult for the hospital staff. She said it was a very, very tough moral issue and she completely supported us, and so on and on. I should say here that I liked Sarita right from the start. She's incredibly nice and Mom's right, she's a great counsellor. I just don't like her bugging me about the grieving teens group. I don't know why, really. Maybe because if I went it would be the first step in letting you go. And I can't face that yet.

Anyway, after Sarita explained everything to us, all the moral and medical issues involved, she helped us make arrangements with a funeral home for you to be cremated. I know. It sounds awful. Can you imagine burning up your own tiny baby? Well, now you know why I wear wacko clothes and wander around in the cemetery looking for the graves of dead babies and writing down their names in my Friends notebook.

Now you know why I'm a freaking lunatic.

Sex

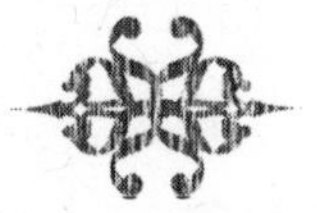

The cemetery vandalism makes the front page of the local paper. There's a picture of the caretaker, Pete Reyburn. Gully's friend. He's standing beside what's left of the burned memorial bench looking grim. He's quoted as saying: "The disrespect shown by these kids is deeply disturbing. For me, for the families who have loved ones here in our cemetery, and for all of Dunlane. I'm a maintenance worker, not a cop. I arrange burials and keep the records and cut the grass. I can't be on site 24/7. The town should seriously consider hiring extra security over the summer."

The mayor's quote is: "Sorry, but Dunlane has no funds for extra security."

Liam feels like crap. Now that the rush is over, he's so sorry. He can't believe what he did. And he's scared of what Ghoul Guy might do next.

At school there's a real buzz. Everybody's talking about the fire in the cemetery. But nobody's admitting anything.

The principal calls a special assembly of the entire student body. They should all be ashamed. They should think about the consequences of this crime. They should give her information. Any information at all, in strictest confidence, blah, blah, blah.

Silence. Loud and clear.

Gully doesn't mention the photo or the article when the paper comes. So Liam doesn't either. But a few days later when they're making dinner, Gully catches him off guard. "My old friend Pete called this afternoon," he says as he lifts the pasta pot from the cupboard.

Liam is chopping onions for tomato sauce. They're using up the last tomatoes from the freezer before this year's crop starts to ripen. "Pete? Oh, you mean that cemetery guy?" He grabs another onion to peel. "The one in the paper?"

Gully fills the pot with water and sets it on the stove to boil. "Yeah, that'd be him." He pulls up a kitchen stool and sits, resting his elbows on the counter where Liam's working. Like he wants to block any attempt at escape. Must be a prison guard move. "He's pretty upset about what happened in the cemetery."

"Yeah, I guess." Liam keeps chopping. He doesn't dare look at Gully. He might miss the onion and cut off his finger. "I mean, of course he would be. He's got no help from the cops, and then he gets stuck with the cleanup."

"Funny thing is," Gully says. He stands and searches in a high cupboard for some pasta. "We used to hang out there too." He opens a box of rotini. "You know, back when me and Pete were kids."

Liam doesn't react. He is so *not* confessing. No matter how rotten he feels. Yeah, what he did was stupid. But it would be even stupider to tell Gully about it. He points to the chopping board and asks, "That enough onions?"

Gully nods. "We used to go to the cemetery to smoke," he says. "And to scare each other shitless with ghost stories, and to make out with girls. Pretty tame stuff, eh?"

Liam rubs at his eyes. They're watering, but only because of the onions. "Times change."

Gully checks the pot but the water isn't boiling yet. "So," he says. "Pete was asking if maybe you know anything?"

"Why would I?" Liam adds the onions to some olive oil heating in a frying pan. They sizzle and he gives them a stir. He starts seeding some peppers.

"Because you're a cool guy. You've probably heard stuff."

Liam adds some spices—Gully's special mix—to the frying onions.

"You can tell me, man to man. I'll understand. Honest. I was young once too, believe it or not."

Liam adds the tomatoes and keeps stirring the sauce. He's not getting fooled by Gully's buddy-buddy thing. He's not confiding that yeah, he was there. That he knows who else was and he'll give up their names. "Does your friend Pete really think I'd be involved in something like that?" He manages to make his voice sound hurt.

He can feel Gully wondering what to do. Come right out and accuse Liam of being in the cemetery that night? The pained look on his face as he adds the pasta to the now boiling water says that he's tempted to avoid confrontation. The water foams up around the pasta and over the edge of the pot, hissing and spitting on the hot stovetop. Gully swears and turns the heat down. "Dunno," he says. "Would you?"

"What? You think I did it?" Liam throws his stirring spoon into the sink. "My *mother* is buried there, for god's sake! And my grandmother too."

"Okay, okay, sorry." Gully tries to wipe off the stovetop. There's a foul burning smell from the wet dishcloth. "But if you do hear anything, will you let me know? Or if you don't want to tell me, you can call Pete. He'll keep your name quiet. These kids have to be stopped."

"Sure. No problem. How long till that pasta's ready?"

After Gully's left for work Liam goes out into the dark garden to check on the tomatoes. Like that will make up for everything. He sees that Gully's put the crushed eggshells he's been saving on the ground around the plants. Apparently they keep the slugs off.

Talk about slugs. He's a shit grandson. He should just leave town. Catch a bus back to the city and take his chances. Lying to Gully isn't fair. Gully's been nothing but good to him.

Liam goes to stand by the spruce tree Gully planted for him. It's a beauty. Not very tall yet, but full and so blue it looks almost silver. Gully must have cared about him a lot, because this is the second tree he planted for him. There's one at his old house too, the one he planted when Liam was born. And he planted them both knowing Liam might never even see them. And he sent all that money to help his mom raise him.

But what did she do with it? Did she quit working as an escort and take a respectable job? Act like a proper mom?

No.

He can't help remembering the first time he'd let himself realize what she actually did. It was just before she started Arabella Investments. One day her friend Laverne came over to get ready for "work" with his mom. They did their hair, plastered on makeup and perfume. And when they went out the door in their revealing clothes and killer stilettos, he'd thought, hey, Laverne looks like a hooker.

And then it hit him. *His mom did too*. Sure, he knew she'd been an exotic dancer. And he knew she worked as an escort now. But she always swore that meant she was just a date. Nothing more. A date for guys in the city on business. A date for guys who'd just moved to town and didn't know anybody yet. A date for guys who had trouble meeting women. She'd always just looked like his mom to him. He'd managed to block out anything else.

But that day he saw her with different eyes. He realized that the "just a date" thing was her way of protecting him. It was a lie they both wanted and needed to believe. But now he had to face the facts. *His mom had sex with guys she didn't know. For money.*

He'd seen the sex ads in the back pages of the tabloids. A lot of ugly images took over his head. It kind of messed him up.

It made him afraid of girls. He swore he'd never have sex without an emotional connection. Without love and respect. Whatever that meant.

When Liam and his mom moved to Mr. Cash & Condo's place, they finally had a talk. Okay, so she wasn't just a date, she said. But being an escort was still just a job. She never worked the street. She only did outcalls, mostly to hotels downtown or near the airport. She offered the girlfriend experience, not the porn-star stuff. She left anything kinky to Laverne. Having their own agency gave them more control and let them make more money. And Arabella Investment's ad was discrete. It didn't have a porn photo of her or Laverne. Just head shots on a black background with gold flowery script: *Invest in your deepest desires*.

She didn't plan on doing it forever. If things worked out with Mr. Cash & Condo, she'd quit. But for then it paid way more than anything else she could do. She hadn't finished high school. She had no career training. But she was a quality escort. She charged top dollar and was always in demand. And they needed the money.

That's the part that always confuses him now. Makes him sad. But missing her is worse. He's starting to wish he had kept something to remember her by that day Laverne packed up his mom's stuff. Because it feels like he's starting to leave her behind already. She's only been dead for three weeks and his life has changed so much.

That fog around her face when he tries to picture her is thicker and thicker every day. It's like she's leaving him to find his own way now. And he's walking down the beach in the opposite direction.

He's walking toward Harmony.

He always figured he might be thirty or something before he could even talk to a girl. Before he met the right one. One who could make him forget that his mom had sex for money. But it was so easy and natural to kiss Harmony. Not dirty at all like he'd worried it might be. He didn't once think about his mom and all those men. Just about Harmony.

All week it's torture to catch glimpses of her around school. Harmony's not in any of his classes. She's just sometimes there in the hall, looking like a different person than she does in the cemetery. At school you'd notice her because of her amazing hair. Not because she's wearing some kind of bizarre costume. So she can't be totally nuts. What happened to make her haunt the cemetery looking for dead babies' graves?

He's wild with wanting, but he doesn't talk to her. He acts like she's got a contagious disease. Which really sucks. But he's so afraid she'll want to talk about what happened at the cemetery. He's already lied to her about his mom. And he's sorry about that. So if Harmony asks him, he'll have to tell her the truth.

He'll have to admit he was at the cemetery with Y4C. He'll have to admit he's a 4. And worst of all, he'll have to admit he started the fire.

And that would be the end of everything.

Tunnel

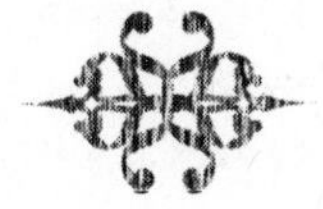

Hey Rue,

Liam's avoiding me again. Oh why, why, why? I'm pretty sure he likes me. I can tell by the way he looks at me at school, before he turns away. As I watch him speeding down the hall in the opposite direction, I can't stop remembering how absolutely perfect it felt to kiss him. And I definitely know he liked the kissing too, so there's only one other reason I can think of why he won't stop to talk to me. He must have helped Y4C vandalize the cemetery.

But how could he do that? His own mother is buried there! He tends her grave with so much love. He waters the grass seed and brings her fresh flowers.

So what was he thinking? Or maybe he wasn't thinking at all, maybe he was acting out his grief and rage at his mother's death. My own experience has taught me that those emotions can make you strange. Sarita says so too. Grief affects your heart, mind, body and spirit. It can make you do things you wouldn't normally do. Things that even a few months ago you'd never have dreamed of. Like joining Y4C and trashing the cemetery. Or dressing up in costumes and flitting about the gravestones communing with dead babies. Scary! If someone had told me last year that that's what

I'd be doing this spring, I'd have laughed my head off. Now it seems I'm just off my head.

I'm sure Sarita, my one-in-a-million counsellor, would have a theory about this, if I ever returned her calls. I'm sure she'd be only too happy to discuss it with me. Before I left the hospital she tried to explain how I might feel in the next while, with my hormones all out of whack from pregnancy and then also something she called the stages of grief setting in, and how I could work through all this in the teen support group. She was right about the hormone hell. Talk about brutal mood swings. But the stages of grief thing? Not so much. She said that when somebody you love dies, first you're in denial, then you get mad, then you get depressed, then you try to bargain with God, and then you finally reach acceptance. But I've come to think that's just the way counsellors wish it would work. In reality, it's way, way more complicated. Except for the bargaining part, which I don't really understand, I've felt all those things, all at once, all the time since you died.

I bled for a month after I lost you, almost as if my body had to keep the wound open. As if my grief had to bleed out of me too, or I'd never be able to fill up my heart with life again. And although I began to recover physically, thanks to a lot of sleep and my parents' care and kindness, I crumbled mentally. Sarita called often to offer follow-up support, but I couldn't or wouldn't tell her how I was feeling. Mostly she talked with Mom and Dad.

And then one day during spring break when the snow was melting and the air was balmy and I just had to be outdoors, I started walking. I had no destination in mind, but somehow ended up at Mount Hope & Glory Cemetery. Not the new part where Liam's mother is buried, with the straight rows and scrawny saplings and elaborate etchings on shiny gravestones and plastic vases filled with ugly fake flowers. No, I found myself in the old part of the cemetery, by the little hill the folks who named the cemetery must have been wishing or pretending was a mountain. Here the gravestones are shaped like simple flat tablets or scrolls or urns, with a few impressive columns on big block bases that mark the resting place of whole families.

But no matter what size they are, the gravestones there are all weathered and mossy and leaning every which way. It's very peaceful and I love to just be there. The wind blows through tall trees and the birds sing and the grass stands long and soft and full of flowers. At first there were snowdrops and crocuses, then daffodils everywhere. And then in late May, just around the time that Liam came to Dunlane, there were forget-me-nots along the riverbank and the lilacs started to bloom.

Along the far edge of the old part of the cemetery there are two rows of big old lilac bushes grown so close together that they form a tunnel. When they were in flower I'd walk up and down on the path inside, pretending it was a portal to another world, to some kind of spiritual place full of sunshine and joy where I like to think you are. And it was one day after I came out of that lilac tunnel that I found the first dead baby grave. Completely by chance. Or not. I noticed that one of the gravestones had a little lamb on top and I went over to take a closer look. It was all covered with lichen but I could still make out the words:

Infant dau. Born April 1888. Died April 1888.

I've learned that often on old gravestones the word daughter is just written "dau." I guess the whole word was too long, too many letters to carve or something. This poor baby didn't even have a name. So I decided to call her Ida, short for Infant dau. Then April for when she was born and died. And then Lamb for the little lamb on her gravestone. Ida April Lamb.

After I found Ida April Lamb, I wanted to search for the graves of other dead babies. And my bizarre hobby just kind of grew from there. I read all about Mount Hope & Glory Cemetery in a book my parents have about the early days of Dunlane. In Victorian times people built cemeteries on a high point of ground to remind themselves of their final destination. Heaven. So I guess that's why they wanted to call it Mount Hope & Glory. And apparently back then people used cemeteries as places to contemplate their own mortality and commune with their departed loved ones. But they also used them like we do parks today, as places to stroll and enjoy nature.

Learning about the Victorian cult of the dead made me consider dyeing all my clothes and even my hair black, and wearing a veil. But the black look is so overdone these days, and dyeing my hair might look like I was trying to copy Mom. Much as I'd love to look like Dazey, I didn't want to go there. So for my next cemetery visit I raided an old trunk and found her prom dress and wore that. Then I started going to the thrift store looking for more fancy dresses I could either wear or refashion. I don't really know why I wanted to dress up for going to the cemetery, but somehow it felt respectful and right. Kind of like updated Victorian mourning clothes.

And now I've started listing, at the back of this notebook, the names of all the dead babies I've found. I love the epitaphs on the gravestones and the old-fashioned names and finding out what age the babies were when they died. A few months, a few weeks, a few hours. I've even found some that simply say: *Stillborn*. Of course lots of the really old, marble gravestones are almost impossible to read. But I take paper and coloured chalk to make rubbings from the most faded ones. That way I can usually make out most of the letters. I read online that some people don't approve of rubbings because they can damage the gravestones, but I'm really careful.

When I visit the dead babies' graves I wonder about their mothers and what they must have suffered, and how they found the time to visit the cemetery with so many other children and a household to look after. But back then, they didn't believe in working on the Sabbath, so I guess that's why Sunday afternoons were a popular time to visit the cemetery. I'm lucky to have hours and hours to sit among the dead and listen to the wind sighing and the birds singing and think about my loss.

Oh Rue. My dear little dead baby.

Here's what's written on the saddest gravestone I've found so far:

Florence Henrietta Bell died Dec. 29, 1883
aged 1 yr 10 mo's.

Alfred Percy Bell died Jan. 8, 1884,
aged 5 mo's.

Safe in the arms of Jesus.

They must have been sister and brother. So their poor mother was way worse off than me. How could anybody stand to lose two babies in less than two weeks?

But sometimes I also wonder if any of the mothers ever felt relief along with their sorrow? Like maybe that mother had nine other kids at home to mind and feed and clothe and maybe she had a brutal husband and no money and maybe she was already pregnant again anyway. Because here's the thing I haven't told anybody. After you died I was so upset, but a couple weeks later I started to feel like an enormous burden had been lifted from me. And I realized that while losing you was the worst thing that had ever happened to me, it was also a huge relief.

Now I don't have to be a single teen mom. I don't have to go through labour and childbirth yet. I don't have to have a baby I'm not ready for. And you don't have to have Jordan/Youth for a father.

So if I'm relieved, knowing I would have managed somehow with my parents' help and financial support, what would those mothers from the past have felt? And yet I know that no matter what, I wish you had lived. I will miss you forever. But since you didn't, I will mourn you and eventually try to get on with my life. That's probably what the mothers of all those dead babies did. They allowed themselves to take to their beds to sob and wail for a few hours and then they got up and mended clothes and scrubbed floors and made supper. On the woodstove or whatever. While all I have to do is get up and go to school. So even with the wonky hormone thing, I've no excuse not to cope better.

It's funny how the words relief and grief kind of rhyme, like they belong together. Some days one is stronger than the other, and then they switch around, like sunshine and rain, with cloudy periods in between. For me anyway. Not for Mom and Dad.

They're devastated by your death. Totally crushed. I honestly don't think they feel any relief at all, only the deepest sadness, even though our lives can sort of go back to something like normal now. But they're in worse shape than I am. I guess they had really come to believe you were their baby. They've completely lost any perspective. Mom's stopped working on your quilt. It's just lying there half-finished in the sewing room. I wish she'd pack it away or something. I hate looking at it when I'm working on my cemetery outfits. But she doesn't go in the sewing room anymore. She doesn't even get dressed most days. She just hides in her office wearing her yoga clothes, online all the time, way more than she used to be for her business. She doesn't talk to Dad or me much, just to Sarita when she calls.

Dad on the other hand is coping by keeping busy. He went to an auction and bought a dining room set with a table, buffet, and twelve chairs to refinish in his workshop. Instead of your cradle. He sold that to a pregnant couple that said they planned to paint it white, so it didn't matter that he hadn't got all the old varnish off yet. I don't think he told them that he hadn't finished it because you died.

My parents and I can't face each other around the house. We pass in the hall or on the stairs and look the other way, like Liam and I do at school. We don't even eat dinner together anymore, which was something they used to insist on. I take my plate up to my room and write in this notebook. Dazey takes hers to her office and goes back online. Noodle takes his out to The Barley Sugar Barn and strips wood, or sometimes plays bits of sad music on his guitar, especially that old Beatles song about letting it be.

I'd love to let it be, but I can't. Because the other thing I feel is guilt. I mean, is it okay to be so relieved? I'd like to ask Sarita this: Does the fact that I'm so relieved not to have you mean that I would have been a bad mother? And should I feel guilty that my parents didn't get the baby they wanted? Because I do. I feel like I've let them down. But even though Sarita gave me her card, I'm afraid to call her. She's sure to be kind and caring like she is with Mom and I'd become dependent on her and want to call her every day.

And then she'd start trying to get me to go to that group for grieving teens and I can't. I just cannot share something so personal with strangers.

I hope maybe someday I can tell Liam. Because he needs to know that I've lost somebody too and I understand what he's going through. And I want him to understand about me, why I care so much about all the dead babies in the cemetery. Why they are so real to me.

And you know what? I just had the best idea. I'm going to do something to honour them, besides writing their names and dates in my Friends notebook. I'm going to have a party for them. A Dead Babies' Birthday Party. Because probably none of them ever had a party in their short lives. I'll hold it in the cemetery, at dawn on the first day of summer. I'll make cupcakes and sew a pair of golden fairy wings to wear. I'll invite Liam to help me celebrate all their missed birthdays.

And then I'll tell him about you.

Ribbons

On Saturday morning Liam heads for the cemetery. He can't stop himself. But he's not going just to visit his mom's grave. He hopes to see Harmony. He's sorry he avoided her all week at school. He needs talk to her. Touch her hair. Kiss her. Feel her kiss him back.

He finds her in the old part of the cemetery, standing beside a huge maple tree. She's dressed as a ballerina or maybe a fairy or something. Her short skirt seems to be made of silver netting, with long multi-coloured ribbons trailing all around. The sight of her shapely legs peeking through almost makes him turn and run. Because how in hell is he supposed to control his urges?

"Come up here." She leaves the tree and climbs a little hill. He follows like a slobbery puppy. She stops by a square block of stone that's covered with greyish-green moss. "This is my favourite gravestone," she tells him. "See if you can read it."

He can't make out all the words, but some of them are: *Alicia Maud. 5 Hrs. Always an Angel.*

There's a stone cherub perched on top of the stone. "Imagine being born and then dying right away." Harmony strokes the cherub's mossy wings. "I love this little statue. I feel so connected to her."

"Yeah, it's cool." What he really wants to say is: I love you. I'd like to be connected to you. I wish you'd touch me like that.

And then he reaches for her.

Harmony steps into his arms.

Oh man, oh man, oh man.

Can she feel his heart beating? It's trying to burst right out of his chest as they kiss and kiss and kiss. He wants her hair down from that tight ballerina bun at the back of her neck. And her netting skirt makes it hard to hold her as close as he'd like. But the lavender leotard she's wearing underneath is soft and smooth in his eager hands.

Then, same as last time, Harmony suddenly breaks away. "Hey," she says, gulping for breath. "I wanted to tell you something. I'm having a Dead Babies' Birthday Party." She moves away from him to touch the little cherub on the gravestone again. "Next Tuesday, that's summer solstice. Here in the cemetery. Want to come?"

"What?" That's about the weirdest thing he's ever heard. Way beyond looking for dead babies' graves and listing their names. Maybe she really is psycho, like Youth and Crime said. Maybe she's even from another planet. "Let me get this straight. You're planning a birthday party, in the cemetery, for all those dead babies?"

"Sure, why not?" She pats the cherub's head. "It's the perfect setting." She spreads her arms to show him the grass and trees and flowers. "I've read that the Victorians used to picnic in burial grounds. And I've heard that nowadays people even hold weddings in cemeteries. So why not a birthday party?"

"I think I might have an exam that day." He doesn't want to hurt her feelings. Even with his lack of girl experience, he can tell she's emotionally fragile. But this idea of hers is too out there. "Yeah, right, I do have an exam. First period."

"So do I." She breaks into a kind of spinning dance, making the multi-coloured ribbons hanging from her skirt twirl out around her bare legs. "But we can still write our exams. The party's at sunrise."

"I'm never awake that early." He'd like to ask her what today's outfit is supposed to be, besides hot enough to make a guy suffer spontaneous combustion. But how to express that without saying the wrong thing and offending her? So he just asks, "Who else is invited?"

Harmony stops dancing and stands very still, arms at her sides. "Nobody. It's just for us and the dead babies." She wraps the ribbons from her skirt around and around her hands. "Don't worry, we'll be safe. Y4C don't get up that early."

What can he say? She's so loony. She's so beautiful. And she just might have the power to save him from self-destruction. "Should I bring presents?"

"Some flowers, if you can." She lets go of her skirt ribbons with a swish so they flutter around her legs again. "And I'm going to bake cupcakes."

"Cupcakes for breakfast?" Who would have thought? "Sweet! I'll be there." So what if she's out of her mind and wears kooky stuff? He loves this Harmony girl. He'll do anything she wants. Go anywhere she asks. Anytime at all.

The memory of kissing her is driving him wild with desire. He's thinking that maybe at the dead babies' birthday party, after they eat the cupcakes, they can kiss some more. Exams don't start until nine, so they'll have lots of time. Maybe they won't even make it to school.

Hey, why wait for Tuesday? Why not right now? He reaches for her again.

Harmony takes his hands. "Sorry, I have to go to an auction with my parents today," she says. "They'll be waiting for me."

"Dressed like that?" The words are out before he can stop them.

She looks like she might cry. She also looks like she might never speak to him again. Like she'll hate him forever.

"Hey, sorry, sorry. You look great and all. But that skirt is, you know, kind of different, and I'm just saying ..." She stays silent so he babbles on, "Oh, god, I'm making it worse, aren't I? How about I just put my other foot in my mouth right now?"

Then she bursts out laughing. "Of course I'm not wearing this when I go out with my parents. What, you think I'm crazy or something?" She shakes her head and turns to go. "See you Tuesday."

He wanders back to the new part of the cemetery and sits by his mom's grave. He can't help noticing that the memorial bench he set on fire is gone. Pete must have taken what was left of it away. But there's still a burnt patch of grass to remind Liam. Christ, why'd he do that?

And why didn't he try harder to convince Gully to have his mom cremated? It's so awful to think of her body down there rotting. Because embalming only slows the process, right? It's so hard to get the image of her lying all stiff and cold in her coffin out of his head.

He tries to bring up his picture of her sitting on that beach log in the yellow raincoat. But he can't see her through the fog. He tries to remember her voice, calling out that it's okay, everything's okay. But all he can hear is the relentless and inhuman sound of waves breaking on the shore.

His mom is slipping away from him. But what's worse is the feeling that he's slipping away from himself. He's no idea who he is anymore. An orphan? Gully's grandson? A 4? He can't believe he burned that memorial bench.

His mom would be so mad at him.

So would Gully.

And Gully's off work for a few days, so he'll be around the house or out in the garden all weekend. The way Liam feels, he might break down and tell Gully everything. So he'll have to spend the rest of the day in his room. Again. He'll have to pretend to be studying. Gully always falls for that one.

But when he gets home they have company. Pete Reyburn, the cemetery caretaker, is sitting in the kitchen. He's a big hefty guy with a salt-and-pepper beard and a bald head.

He and Gully are drinking coffee and arguing about something. Liam's sure that something is him. Pete probably came over to grill him about the cemetery. Or the vandalism on Main Street. Or whatever he can make Liam tell him about the youth crime problem in Dunlane. Not a chance.

"Smells good," Liam says as he enters. Gully has bacon frying and eggs scrambling and toast toasting.

The conversation stops. There's an awkward silence and both Gully and Pete look guilty. Strange. Why would that be? Isn't Liam supposed to be the guilty one?

He's sure they were talking about him. But whatever they were saying, it's obvious they aren't going to tell him. He so does not need this.

Gully jumps up to serve the food. But Pete shakes his head and jumps up too. "Sorry, gotta run." He pours his unfinished coffee down the sink. "Nice to see you, Liam." He's gone before Gully can set his plate down.

"What's up with that?" Liam asks. "How come Pete didn't stick around to eat?" He's starving and he digs in.

"Oh, Pete just stopped by to see how the tomatoes are doing." Gully's answer comes way too fast. "I always give him a ton and he likes to watch them grow." Yup, Gully's hiding something. That's a complete lie. They weren't even in the garden. And any other day he'd tell Liam to cook his own breakfast.

"Really? I thought maybe he was here to question me, because of him calling the other day. But then he took off so fast."

"No, no." Gully starts making some fresh coffee. "That's not what he wanted."

Liam sets down his fork. "But it wasn't about the tomatoes, either, was it?"

"What makes you say that?" Gully's look tells him not to push it.

"Just a feeling. I mean, you guys weren't exactly out in the garden. And he's never come by before. At least, not when I've been here."

"Let it go." Prison guard growl. "Just forget it."

Now Liam really wants to know what's going on. "Was it about me? Because it sure felt like it."

No response. He finishes his breakfast and waits. The longer Gully doesn't speak, the more panicked Liam feels. He's sure they were talking about him being a vandal. Probably he should just get this over with and confess. "Gully? What's the story?"

Gully clears the table and fills the sink with hot soapy water. Starts washing the dishes. Keeps his back to Liam.

"Pete thinks I was at the cemetery that night, doesn't he?" But if that's why he was here, then Gully must have been defending Liam. Otherwise Pete would have stayed. Ouch. It makes things even harder to know that Gully trusts him. "I have a right to know if you guys were dissing me."

"That is *not* what he wanted." Gully turns and glances around, as if Pete might be lurking somewhere. "He told me something, and he wanted to tell you, too. But I wouldn't let him."

"Why not? What's the big deal?"

Gully comes and stands in front of Liam's chair. Places his hands firmly on Liam's shoulders. "You really want to know?"

Liam looks up into Gully's pained face. "Yeah, I do."

"Okay, just remember you asked for this." Gully puts more pressure on Liam's shoulders so he can't escape.

Liam tries anyway. But Gully's hold is too strong. "Okay, I give up. So just say it already."

"There's no easy way to tell you."

"I can deal."

"You think? Because you're not going to like this." Gully spits out his words like they're poison pills he's swallowed by mistake. "Thing is, Pete's your father."

Guilty

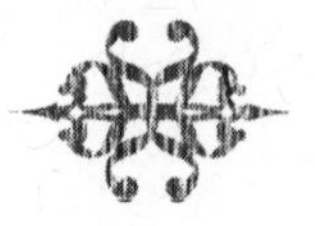

Liam gapes at Gully in disgust and denial. *Pete Reyburn is his father*? No way. No way in the world! Pete Reyburn, the cemetery caretaker with the beer gut, the faded hippie beard and the bald head? The guy who's as old as his grandfather? *He's Liam's Dad?*

Liam lunges to punch Gully.

"Take it easy, kid." Gully holds him down on the chair. "I know it's a shock, but if it's any help, it was news to me too." Sounds like he really means that. Like he's as upset as Liam.

Liam still can't process the news. He struggles to break free, but Gully has way more power. Liam is taller, but he doesn't have anywhere near the muscle. Gully works out five days a week and it shows. And being a prison guard, he has a lot of experience restraining guys.

Gully holds on tight while Liam bellows out his rage. Sounds like he's being murdered. Feels like it too. All those years believing what his mom said about his no-name sperm-donor father. Believing there weren't any details to share. Yeah, he'd known she might be making that up. But he sure as hell didn't expect somebody who went to school with his grandfather.

He didn't expect Pete frigging Reyburn!

He wishes Pete *had* been there about the cemetery vandalism. He could have stood that. He'd have admitted his guilt and taken his punishment. But he doesn't deserve this sudden surprise father thing. It's completely unfair. And unbelievable.

What's he supposed to do now?

It's not like he's always wanted to know who his father was. He's never really cared. He had his mom. And she was enough. He didn't need a father before she died. He doesn't want one now.

Why should he care about a guy who didn't care about him? A guy who never even tried to meet his son? A guy who didn't pay child support? Sperm donor or one-night stand, either was fine with Liam. Either made it easy to hate the guy.

After all his shouting it feels like he's frothing at the mouth when he finally gets some words out. "What made him decide to tell us now?"

"Liam." Gully releases his hold, pulls up a chair and sits down. "Pete swears he really loved her. He wanted them to get married. But she wasn't interested. Called him a big mistake."

"And so he just let her run away to the city and become a—"

"And so he respected that she didn't want him around, and that she didn't want to tell you about him." Gully gives Pete's excuses as fast as he can. "But now she's gone, he wants you to know that he cares."

"He wants me to know he cares?" The words slobber out of Liam's mouth. "But she was only seventeen! And he must have been what? Like forty-five or something?"

Gully makes a groaning sound like a wounded animal. "Yeah, I know, that's kind of hard to take." He moves as if to hug Liam, then pulls back and massages his shoulders instead. "But he says it was mutual. He didn't take advantage of her, or, you know, rape her or anything."

Rape her? Oh god. He never even thought of that. "And you believe him?"

Gully stops rubbing Liam's shoulders. Looks him right in the eye. But not with his prison guard glare. With grandfatherly love. "Actually," he says, "strange as it might sound, I do. I've known Pete forever. He's a good person."

"So she knew him because he was your friend?"

"No," Gully says. "I mean, she did know I knew him, but mostly he was her history teacher. He wasn't always the cemetery caretaker, you know. He just started that job after he retired."

"He was her teacher?" Liam remembers his English teacher, Ms. Smythe, looking at him funny all those times. He'd thought she was just disapproving of Monica Hall having a baby so young. But maybe she knew who the father was. Maybe she knew that a DDHS history teacher had abused a student's trust and gotten her pregnant. "Isn't that, like, illegal or something?"

Gully grimaces. "It's not something Pete's proud of. And yes, I guess there could have been charges. She was underage, and he was in a position of authority." He stands and paces around the kitchen. "If I'd known at the time ... but I didn't. And he swears it was mutual. Which doesn't excuse him, but he might not be completely to blame. You have to realize that Monica was seductive. Well, I guess you're aware of that. Oh, and he says that he sent her money every month too."

He did? This is way too much. Liam definitely can't deal. He needs to get out of here. Away from Gully and this shocking, unwelcome news. Away from the idea that he's related to Pete. That the cemetery caretaker is his fucking father. "I've got exams all next week." Liam gets up to leave the kitchen. "I have to study."

Of course he can't study at all. Instead he checks out the photo of his mom as Miss Dunlane 1996. He's wondering if the guy driving the convertible she's riding in could be Pete. And he's right. He didn't recognize him before, but he does now. Pete looks about fifty pounds lighter and he still has hair, but it's definitely him. Liam wants to rip the frame off the wall and smash it. Tear out that photo and shred it.

He paces around the room like Gully was doing in the kitchen. Like a caged beast. If only he could go swim laps somewhere to calm himself down. But all he can do is punch his pillow until his fists hurt.

He's trying to stop himself going to find Pete. But not to confront him about being his father. To beat the crap out of him. So what if Pete's bigger and probably a better fighter? Liam's so pissed he knows he can take him.

And then Pete won't have an office in the cemetery anymore. He'll be living there. Under the ground. Just like Liam's mom.

He wishes he could call Harmony. But even if he had her number, she's not home. She's out with her parents. So she couldn't come over and comfort him. Or stop him doing something he knows he'll regret.

Like killing Pete.

He has to chill. So he thinks about kissing Harmony. But it doesn't work. It excites him and adds to his pain. It reminds him of his mom and Pete. And that is just too gross. No wonder she didn't want to tell Liam about his father. He's so *old*! He's as ancient as Gully.

And Liam has the sick feeling that he kind of looks like Pete. The height and the eyes. And guessing from Pete's beard, back when he had hair it was as dark as Liam's.

For god's sake Mom! Weren't there any guys your own age?

There's another cemetery party tonight. Maybe he'll go and do some serious damage. Wouldn't it be better to trash some gravestones than give Pete a beating? But he knows either is a bad idea. He has to restrain himself. And as long as Gully's home, he can probably stay in control. Having Gully around makes him feel safe.

They turn on the TV after dinner, but keep seeing replays of the hockey fans rioting in Vancouver after the Stanley Cup final. "Bunch of morons," Gully says, scowling at the TV, then at Liam. "Shit for brains."

Then the phone rings. There's an emergency at the prison. Somebody got stabbed. Now Millhaven is locked down. Gully is needed ASAP.

Maybe he should get Gully to handcuff him before he speeds away in his truck. Because that's it for Liam. There's nothing to stop him now. He has to get out of the house. And there's only one place he wants to go.

Next thing he knows he's running to the cemetery. Ghoul Guy needs to punish Pete. Thinking about those hockey fans rioting and the prison lockdown urges him on. It's time to take action. He's pulsing with dangerous energy.

Bring it on!

The party's already wild when he gets there. Everybody's drunk or high or both. Ranting and raving, "Youth 4 Crime! Youth 4 Crime! *Y4C4EVR!*"

They've already wrecked a lot of gravestones. Now they're ripping the plaques from memorial trees. They're breaking off branches and trying to pull the young trees down. The dogs are growling and racing about biting the fallen branches.

For a split second Liam remembers the tree Gully planted for him. That blue spruce in the back yard. How would he feel if somebody destroyed it?

Part of him knows he should get out of there. Try to find Harmony. She's probably home by now and he knows where she lives. Maybe she could come over to Gully's and help him smash that photo of his mom and Pete. Gully would be mad, but not as mad as he'll be if Liam joins Y4C's rampage in the cemetery.

Another part of him knows he should alert Pete. Or call the cops. Tell them to get down here.

But a bigger part of him wants to stay. He's had a taste of being bad and now he wants more. Ghoul Guy craves another rush.

Sure, he knows it's stupid. Really, really stupid. But he doesn't care.

He doesn't touch the memorial trees though. He heads straight for the caretaker's restored chapel office. Pete doesn't live here—he only uses it for a workspace. But still. This is going to be almost as good as beating him up.

Pete should suffer as much as Liam has. The guy took advantage of a seventeen-year-old girl. His student. The daughter of one of his childhood friends. And then all those years, he never once tried to meet his son.

Not that Liam wanted to meet his father, but Pete should have tried. So what if he sent money? He never once came to visit. He never even came over to Gully's the few times Liam and his mom were there.

The town of Dunlane spent thousands of dollars restoring the historic chapel for the caretaker's office. Liam remembers Pete blabbing on about it the day of his mom's burial. He said it took ten years for the Friends of Mount Hope & Glory Cemetery to raise the funds.

It only takes ten minutes to trash the place. As soon as kids see what he's doing they come join him. They're so into it. But Liam's the leader.

They kick down the door. Break the stained glass windows. Knock over the furniture and empty Pete's desk and files. They tear up paperwork and stuff it in the toilet. Flush it until it water floods everywhere.

Then they piss all over everything. Some kids puke. Others do worse. Pete's office is a stinking vile mess.

But that's not enough for Ghoul Guy.

There's something else he has to do.

He runs to his mom's grave.

He stands there in the darkness, panting and sweating. Wondering about the prison lockdown. Is there a riot? Is it contained?

Maybe that's where he'll end up. In prison.

It seems like he must be crying or something because he can't read his mom's name and dates. But he knows by heart the words on the pink granite gravestone with the birds and butterflies carved around the edges.

Monica Susan Hall, 1979 – 2011
Dearly Beloved. Always Remembered.
Rest in Peace.

His mom was seventeen and she willingly had sex with some guy more than twice her age? A friend of her father? Then she ran away to the city to have his baby on her own? And become a sex trade worker? An exotic dancer and then an escort?

Pete sent money, just like Gully. All those years. But she still sold herself.

Why Mom? Why? Why? Why?

And then it hits him. His mom was always talking about quitting Arabella Investments. Especially after she met Mr. Cash & Condo. She said Laverne could get a new partner or even run the business herself. But she never went through with it. She never did quit.

Maybe ordinary life seemed boring to her, after working in such a high-risk job. Maybe that's why she went out that last night. Not because they needed the money. And not even because she wanted to see Mr. Cash & Condo. But because she needed the thrill.

She was addicted to risk!

Just like her son.

Somebody hands him a can of black spray paint. And then he goes wild with rage and grief. But he doesn't put: *Y4C4EVR!*

He puts: *Bitch! Slut! Whore!*

All over his mom's gravestone.

Ashes

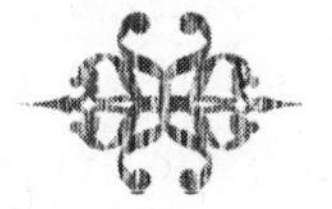

Hey Rue,

Today was a big day for me. I met Liam in the cemetery and then I went to an auction with Noodle and Dazey. More about Liam later. I want to tell you about the auction first. See, Mom and Dad and I used to go out together all the time, looking for stuff for The Barley Sugar Barn or for eBay. But we haven't been anywhere since we lost you. We haven't been out as a family at all. None of us have the heart for restaurants or movies, garage sales, flea markets or auctions. So it was a super big deal that we went. And I have to say that it was Sarita the helpful counsellor who made it happen.

She told my parents she wanted to buy a rolltop desk and a pine blanket-box and some botanical prints, since she's got that old house down by the river now to furnish with antiques. But with her heavy caseload she doesn't have time to go around to antique stores or sales, so would they be willing to act as her agents and look for stuff for her, them being such experts and all.

Well, they couldn't resist that. Not only could they help Sarita, who's helped them so much, but it was a great excuse to get back onto the auction circuit. To put the past behind them and start getting on with their lives. And they wanted me to come along, just like I used to, even if I was supposed to be studying for final exams. Okay, so it wasn't all that hard to convince me either. Who wants to spend a spectacular June Saturday indoors studying?

The auction was actually an estate sale, held at a century stone farmhouse in the country, the kind of place that's only been owned by one family and no one has ever thrown anything out. And once we were there, I realized how much I've missed the thrill of auctions—signing-in for our bidding number, looking over all the lots to see what we want to bid on, staying calm when the bidding starts and then jumping in at the last second and getting what we want for almost nothing. Or maybe hearing the auctioneer's voice rattle faster and faster, pushing the bidding higher and higher, out of our price range, until we hear that final "Sold!" and wonder who on earth would bid that high?

So yeah, the auction was better than studying. Not as much fun as old times, but that was mostly because Mom kept seeing things like a wooden rocking horse and an antique dollhouse that she would have bid on for you and that made her cry. But we all felt the rush when Dad started bidding on the perfect desk for Sarita. He didn't get it though, because it was so very perfect that someone else bid more than she wanted to pay. But still, the challenge of hunting down the right piece for a buyer who is now also sort of a family friend has taken hold. There's a big sale at an auction house in Kingston next weekend and we've already made plans to go. Mom says the online catalog shows some prints that she knows Sarita will love.

Now back to Liam. He showed up at the cemetery this morning just like I hoped. I wore a fabulous ballet fairy costume that must have really knocked him out, because he couldn't seem to stop staring at it. Well, staring at the rainbow of ribbons I stitched to the tutu skirt that drift down around my legs and twirl when I move. But anyway, the other big thing that happened today was—guess what? I kissed him again! I mean I really, really kissed him and it felt really, really good. And this time I only stopped myself because I knew Noodle and Dazey were waiting to go to the auction, and I didn't want them driving around the cemetery looking for me in our old green van that has "The Barley Sugar Barn" painted in huge gold curlicued letters on one side and "Sweet Deals" in silver on the other.

I might introduce Liam to my parents sometime, but not yet. I have to be sure about him, and that means telling him about you. So after I showed him my favourite gravestone with the little stone cherub, I invited him to my Dead Babies' Birthday Party, which is when I plan to talk to him about you. At first he seemed to think the party was kind of a strange and morbid idea. Which I guess it is. He squinted up his gorgeous hazel eyes and took a step back from me. But then I told him about the cupcakes I'm going to bake and he said he'd come.

It's going to be so great, Rue. My plan is to read out the names of all the dead babies I've written down in the back of this notebook, and then we'll celebrate their short tragic lives by eating the cupcakes. And after that we'll kiss again. And then I'll try to get up my nerve to tell him about you and if he's okay with that, then maybe he can meet my parents. And I'll show him where I keep you.

I hope you like your earthly home. I know its not exactly the nursery Mom and Dad were redecorating for you, but it's the best I could do under the circumstances. After I recovered from the miscarriage, well, physically anyway, I had to decide what to do with your ashes. I know some people thought it was wrong, like immoral or something, cremating a fetus one week short of being a person and then wanting to keep the remains. Or cremains, as some people call them. I overheard one of the nurses telling Mom that what was left of you would be almost nothing, more like a fluff of dust from under a bed. But both Mom and Sarita the grief counsellor said so what, if that's what Harmony wants? So we brought your fluffy-dusty cremains home in a little plastic baggy like you were pot or something, which seemed very cold and heartless but was the most convenient way to carry you until I could decide where to keep you. I knew I didn't want an infant urn or a memory box like the funeral home showed us, and for sure I didn't want you made into a keepsake picture frame or jewellery or whatever like I saw advertised online. That stuff all seemed so stupid and expensive, not to mention creepy and final.

I had an idea that I might find something I'd like in The Barley Sugar Barn and so I looked around out there. I almost gave up though. I didn't want to keep you in a sugar bowl or a candy dish or a wooden cigar box. But then I found the perfect thing. It's a flat cut-glass box with a sterling silver lid, only about the size of a small bar of soap. It's part of a lady's dresser set, and has a matching perfume bottle and hand mirror and hair brush. Dad said the box was probably for keeping rings or earrings in, and that I could have it. He could still sell the rest of the set without it. And even better, the name of the lady who once owned the set was engraved on the silver lid in elegant script:

Rue.

And when I sprinkled your puff of remains inside and put that lid back on, that's when I knew I would call you Rue. It's perfect—an old-fashioned name meaning a bitter herb and also meaning regret.

Your little glass box is the only outfit you'll ever wear. I know that sounds demented, like I've completely lost my mind. And maybe I have. But I can't help remembering all those darling baby clothes I looked at online and how now you'll never need them. You don't need anything or anybody at all.

I wish you could tell me what I should do with you. Bury you in the back yard? Scatter you to the wind? Keep you in my room? I can't decide and I guess it doesn't really matter, does it? For now I carry you with me in your little glass box in my patchwork bag, along with my Friends notebook, whenever I go to the cemetery. One day I set you down beside the stone cherub on Alicia Maud McRory's gravestone. I almost left you there. It seemed a good place for you, her being the daughter of the family whose house we live in and all.

But in the end I couldn't leave you. I put you back in my bag and carried you home, where I tucked you in my bottom drawer, under the pieces of fabric and bits of ribbon and fancy buttons I collect for costumes.

For the Dead Babies' Birthday Party I'll have to bake the cupcakes the night before, so they'll be cool enough to frost before I go to bed. I've found a great recipe for vegan cupcakes online that should be perfect. I'll have to set my alarm too. I told Liam to come to the cemetery at six and I don't want to be late. The cupcakes will be chocolate but I'll cover them with vanilla frosting so the coloured sprinkles I bought to decorate them with will show up better. Babies like bright colours. I've even got a wicker picnic basket of Mom's to carry the cupcakes in. I wish we could have ice cream too, but it would melt. I'll bring candles though, one for each cupcake, and one cupcake for each dead baby.

I'm going to wear Dazey's lime-green prom dress again, because that's what I was wearing the first time I met Liam. And I've already made the fairy wings. I actually found a useable pair, part of kid's costume, at the Goodwill store. I cut the netting off the frame and recovered the wings with gold organza that I bought from the remnant bin at the fabric shop, since I couldn't find what I wanted in any old dresses and I wanted the wings to be just right. Oh, and I meant to tell you, when I was stitching the wings I folded away your half-finished quilt. It upset me too much looking at it. I'm sure Mom won't mind. She'll be glad I tidied up the sewing room. No, that's wishful thinking. She won't even notice. She'll walk right by the sewing room, go into her office and boot up her laptop. Honestly, I think she's having an Internet affair or something, she's always online.

Anyway, the wings are perfect! I love how they turned out. They fit over my shoulders like a weightless backpack. When I tried them on I felt like I really might be able to fly. And they look awesome with the dress. I'll have to think of something special to do with my hair too. I am sooooo excited! I can't wait for my Dead Babies' Birthday Party.

Cupcakes

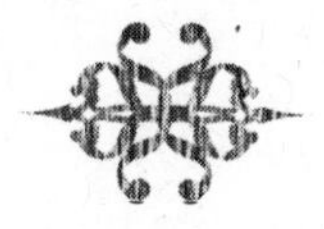

Gully phones home to say the prison situation is serious. They've called in help from everywhere possible to stop the riot. He won't be back anytime soon, probably not for a couple of days. Liam should look after himself. Study hard and ace his exams. And oh yeah, please don't forget to water the tomatoes, they need to be kept evenly moist.

Liam drags himself to school on Monday and Tuesday. Writes his exams in a daze. Everybody's talking about what went down at the cemetery.

Everybody but Liam. He's busy worrying how Gully and Pete will react when they find out he was involved. And then trying to block out what he did. Trying to pretend he wasn't there.

Sorry now that he was.

How could he have wrecked his so-called father Pete's office?

How can Pete be his father anyway? It's so not fair to suddenly find that out. And who cares if Gully says Pete's okay? The guy's a dickhead. He slept with his student and got her pregnant. He knew about his kid but never even tried to meet him. So he deserves Liam's revenge.

But how could Liam have graffitied his mom's grave?

For that he is deeply embarrassed and truly sorry.

When he sees Harmony coming down the hall towards him, Liam slinks the other way. As usual. He can't face her.

Then she rounds a corner unexpectedly and plants herself in front of him. There's no escape. But instead of questions about where he was on Saturday night, she says, "Don't forget my Dead Babies' Birthday Party. Tomorrow morning. Bright and early."

Even though her party idea is beyond weird, she looks completely sane today at school. No bizarre dress, just jeans that fit perfectly. A loose white shirt that kind of floats over a pink tank top. Liam wants to kneel down and kiss her feet. Run away with her and live happily ever after. "But didn't you see the paper? Some bad stuff happened at the cemetery. Y4C trashed it. You don't want to go there."

"Of course I do," she says. "I mean, I saw that disgusting picture of what they did to the caretaker's office, but Y4C don't scare me. They don't own the cemetery."

"Um, actually, they might think they do." The look on her face makes him quickly add, "But if you still want me to come, I will."

Yeah, he'll be there. But then what? What's she going to do when she finds out he was part of all that destruction? When she sees what he did to his mom's gravestone? Because the one thing he knows for sure is that Harmony, like Gully and Pete, will eventually find out.

It's only a matter of time.

Maybe Pete will come by the house looking for him. He must know Gully's at Millhaven. So many people in town work at the prison that everybody always hears what's going on there. Pete could easily figure out that Liam's on his own and drop in to check on him.

Pete doesn't show up though.

Liam is alone with his guilt. All night long. It's not hard to wake up for the Dead Babies' Birthday Party, because he hasn't been asleep. He's been awake for hours wondering what to do. If he wants Harmony to like and trust him, he has to tell her everything.

But he can't. What if she thinks he's worse than Youth? What if she hates him?

She asked him to bring flowers so he picks some daisies from Gully's garden. He reaches the cemetery just as the sky is brightening. Finds Harmony wandering around the old part. Her costume for the party is the long green prom dress from the first day he met her. Her hair is up in a fancy braid on top of her head, which shows off the pair of sparkly gold wings she's wearing on her back.

She's carrying a basket of cupcakes and talking to herself. No, she's muttering and weeping like a mad thing. It sounds like she's saying, "My baby, my baby, my poor sweet baby."

"Harmony!" When she turns, Liam opens his arms wide, as if he's got wings, too. "I'm here."

She runs into his embrace. Which makes her picnic basket go flying, spilling cupcakes and candles everywhere. He ignores the mess and closes his arms around her. Holds her tight. "Hey, hey, it's okay, everything's going to be okay." He's not so sure though.

"They took my baby," she sobs. "They broke her! My baby, my baby, my baby!"

She points to the grave where the little stone cherub used to be. The gravestone is lying on the ground. The cherub is broken off. Smashed to pieces.

What the hell? That must have happened when he was trashing Pete's office. If only he'd known. He'd definitely have made sure Harmony didn't come here today. "I'm so sorry." He puts the daisies he brought down by the broken cherub. "Let's get out of here."

Harmony keeps wailing, "My baby, my baby, my poor dead baby."

"Hey, it's okay, it's okay." He has to tell her everything now, even if she hates him for it. He knows how much that cherub meant to her, and he's so ashamed of what Y4C's done.

He picks up the cupcakes even though they're all smushed and covered with dirt and grass and stuff. "Don't worry, these still look awesome," he says, trying to arrange them as nicely as possible in the basket. He wipes the sticky frosting off his hands onto his jeans. Leads her to his mom's grave.

The words are still there on her stone: *Bitch! Slut! Whore!*

"Oh my god!" Harmony clutches at her heart. "Oh my god! How could they do that?"

"*They* didn't."

"Of course they did! Y4C are so evil! I hate them!"

"Harmony." He makes himself look at what he did. How could he ever have been so stupid and thoughtless?

Sure, he had his reasons.

But he has no excuses.

"Harmony, I have to tell you something." If he'd had anything to eat this morning he'd be barfing it up now. As it is he kind of chokes the words out, like bitter green bile. "*I* did it."

She steps closer to the gravestone, reaching out to trace the butterflies and birds carved around the edge. "No, you didn't." She shakes her head so hard her fairy wings tremble. "You couldn't have," she says. "You're not like that."

Liam feels like he might pass out. Her trust leaves him breathless. Her belief in him is worse than if she'd run away screaming.

And even worse is the temptation to keep this gift that he doesn't deserve. Let her blame Y4C. Let her keep thinking he's a nice guy.

But he can't stop the words spewing out. "Yeah, I did." His voice heaves up from deep inside him. "Me. Her son. I wrote that stuff."

Harmony looks like he's punched her. "But," she says. "But why?"

"Because," he says. "Because I'm an asshole. And I lied about her too. She never worked in a flower store."

"She didn't?"

"No."

"What did she do?"

"My mom," he says. "My mom was a sex worker. She and her friend Laverne ran an escort agency. They called it Arabella Investments, so it sounded like a financial firm, and it was very classy and upscale. But she worked as a prostitute." There. He's said it. He's told her.

"Oh," Harmony says.

"But you know what? You don't need to feel sorry for her. She wasn't a drug addict, or controlled by a pimp, or any of the other stereotypes that everyone believes. She was, you know, nice. And she was a successful businesswoman making more money than she could at anything else. End of story."

Well, the end of what he's telling her today. He can't bear to admit how his mom let all that money she made, and all that money Gully and Pete sent, slip through her fingers. How Gully said he'd told her to invest in an education fund for Liam, but she didn't. She spent it on herself: cosmetic surgery and designer clothes and shoes. There's nothing left for her kid.

Harmony picks up the basket of broken cupcakes and examines them. Tries to smooth the frosting with her fingers. Gives up and sets the basket back down. "Did she really die in a car crash?"

"Yeah, that part was true. But what I didn't tell you was that she was walking alone at four in the morning. Wearing a skimpy dress, fishnet stockings and stilettos."

"Ah." Harmony pokes at the cupcakes again. "But did they ever find out who hit her?"

"Not yet. The police said she was in the wrong place at the wrong time. It was just, you know, random. There's an ongoing investigation, but they might never know what really happened. My grandfather says that we'll just have to live with the questions."

Harmony sits down on his mom's grave. "That's so sad." She takes off her fairy wings so she can lean back against the gravestone. As she stretches out her legs he can see that her toenails are now polished a glittery gold. He guesses that's to match the wings.

"She always took a cab. *Always*. So I don't know what she was doing that night. And I have to accept that I never will." He sits down beside Harmony. With both their backs against the gravestone they're covering most of the spray paint.

Harmony takes his hand. "What you did to your mom's gravestone, that was a rotten thing to do."

"I know, I know." He has the stuffed up feeling that means he's going to start bawling. He's so ashamed of that graffiti. He inhales and holds his breath. Scrunches up his eyes to stop the tears. When it's safe to exhale he says, "I'm sorry. Oh god, I'm so, so sorry."

"I know," Harmony says softly. "I'm sure she'll forgive you."

"But will you?" That's far more important. His mom would understand. But will Harmony? It's asking a lot for her to be okay with what he did. "Will you forgive me?"

She lets go of his hand, picks up her wings and pretends to make them fly. "Honestly," she says, "I don't really know. Give me some time, okay?" She rests the wings on the ground. "And I'll give you some time too, because now it's my turn to confess."

"Huh?" What could she possibly have to confess? "You already told me about Youth, and being at that Halloween party."

"But there's more," she says. "See, the real reason I wanted to have a party for the dead babies is that, um ..." She starts to weep again, choking out the words, "My baby, my baby, my poor sweet baby."

He holds her for a while, rocking her like she's an infant herself.

When she calms down she says, "Okay. Here's the thing. My baby would have been born in July."

"What?"

"My baby," she repeats. "She should have been born in July. See, I got pregnant last fall with Youth, when he was still called Jordan, by mistake at that Halloween party, in the caretaker's office. So I'm kind of glad it got wrecked because it had really bad memories for me. Anyway, by the time I realized I was pregnant, I hated Jordan and his stupid gang. Then he started calling himself Youth and he hooked up with my ex-best-friend Christine. I didn't care about all that, but I didn't know what to do about the baby and I kind of let my parents talk me into keeping her. It seemed like the best idea at the time, you know?"

Harmony pauses. Waits for him to react to what she's told him. But what should he say? It's hard to process this new information. While he's trying to form some words she gives up and goes on. "But then at nineteen weeks I miscarried. And after that I started listing all the dead babies' names and then you came along."

He picks up her wings and flutters them around like she did. Anything to buy some time. He knows it's really, really important to say the right thing. And he so wants to say whatever it is she wants to hear. But he's no clue what that might be. This is even more confusing than finding out that Pete is his father.

Finally he holds her wings still in the silence between them. "Do you wish you were still having that baby?"

She sighs. A long, soft sigh full of pain and sorrow. "Yes and no. Yes because I'd come to want her. And no because I'm way too young. I didn't ever love Jordan and I didn't want to have his child. It was my first time and I was stupid and I got burned."

"You know what?" He flaps the wings around again. "I've never done it. I mean, because of my mom and all, I never wanted to. Well, I wanted to, but I couldn't imagine ever being with a girl."

She wipes her eyes and smiles. "We can take it slow."

His heart stops beating. Restarts, double time.

She slips her golden fairy wings back on.

"Time to honour the dead babies."

"Oh god. You're not going to sing, are you?"

She pulls her notebook out of her bag. "Hey, I never thought of that. But nah, just because I'm called Harmony, doesn't mean I can sing." She stands, faces the old part of the cemetery, inhales deeply like she's onstage or something and says, "Happy Birthday, Dead Babies." Then she reads off all their names.

When she's done she settles beside Liam on his mom's grave. "So here we are," he says. "You with your dead babies and me with my dead mom. We're stuck in a land of death."

"And cupcakes," Harmony says, pointing to the basket. "It's actually a land of death and cupcakes."

Liam reaches for a crumbly cupcake and lifts it to his mouth. "Then let's eat."

Later

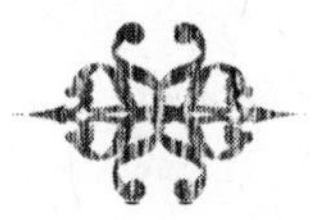

Hey Rue,

Something terrible happened. Liam told me at school that Y4C had vandalized the cemetery on Saturday night, and I did see it in the paper, but I didn't realize how bad it was. When I got there before dawn on summer solstice with my basket of cupcakes for the Dead Babies' Birthday Party I was shocked. I saw that they'd wrecked my favourite gravestone, the one for Alicia Maud McRory. They'd knocked it over and the little stone cherub was broken off and all in pieces. I thought I'd die when I saw it. I didn't know what to do. I wanted to take it home for Dad to fix, because he knows how to restore things, he's always touching up cracks and chips in old china. He can make anything look like new. But I could see the stone cherub was beyond repair. So I was wandering around weeping and wailing and gnashing my teeth when Liam showed up.

And then I ran to him and spilled the cupcakes! I didn't even think, I was just so glad to see him and we crashed into each other and I lost hold of the basket and the cupcakes rolled all over the ground and most of them broke or got squashed. And they'd looked so good when I left the house. I'd spent hours the night before getting them just right. Liam tried to pick the cupcakes up and put them back in the basket and they were such a mess but I was so impressed that he bothered to do that. I was too upset and would have just left them lying there for the squirrels to eat. And then he kind of pulled me to his mother's grave and showed me the worst graffiti I've ever seen.

I can't even write it down here, it was so vile. I was furious with Y4C and started going on about how I hate them and what they do but Liam said no, that he'd done it. I have to admit I was totally shocked, maybe more than I've ever been in my entire life, even when I found out I was pregnant. But then he explained why he was so mad at his mother, and then I was even more shocked. He says she was a prostitute! But I know it's not my place to judge anybody, especially not a single mom who had her baby when she was a teenager and tried to look after him on her own.

I couldn't help thinking about how my own mom gave her baby up without even seeing him, and what might have happened if she'd kept him, and how I would have coped if you had lived. Probably Liam's mom just did what she had to do to survive.

Thinking about all that kind of freed me to tell him about you. And guess what? He didn't freak out at all. Maybe because he'd just admitted to the shameful way he'd treated his mother's gravestone. And then we sort of talked about sex and agreed to not rush into anything and then it seemed like we should finish the party.

It was a glorious morning as the pastel pinks and mauves of the dawn sky brightened into a first day of summer blue. Liam actually listened, or pretended to, while instead of singing "Happy Birthday" I read off the names and dates of all the dead babies. And then we ate the cupcakes. Well, what was left of them. We didn't bother lighting the candles because there was nowhere to stick them with the cupcakes all in pieces and I'd somehow forgotten matches. The edible bits were all sticky and pretty gross but they tasted great. In the end I think it was the best birthday party ever. But probably that's because we both felt so relieved to have shared our secrets and confessed everything.

Okay, not quite everything. I didn't actually tell Liam that I carry you around in an antique glass box with your name engraved on the silver lid. Maybe when I know what I'm going to do with you I'll show you to him first. Or not. The most important thing was telling him about you at all. But I have a funny feeling that I'm going to stop carrying you with me to the cemetery. In fact I'm probably going to stop going to the cemetery altogether, unless I go with Liam to visit his mother's grave. Because I feel like I'm almost ready to let the dead babies go. I've recorded their names and given them a party and now it's time to stop obsessing about them.

And here's another surprise. My Mom and I are kind of talking again like we used to. I went into her office when I came home from the cemetery this morning, pretending I wanted to borrow a pen, because I had my last exam this afternoon. But really I just needed to see her. I've missed her so much. I wanted to tell her about the dead babies and the broken cherub and Liam and everything, and maybe get back to the way we were before all this happened.

She took one look at me and said I certainly hope you're not wearing that outfit to school. I didn't even realize I still had on her old prom dress and the golden fairy wings. But I like your hair done up like that, she said. It's very becoming. And then I said, becoming what? And we both laughed. That's one of our old jokes that I started the first time she ever said that to me. I'd never heard the expression before and took it literally. I thought she meant I was like a transformer or something. And then she said, sweetheart, you are so beautiful. I love you so much. Oh and by the way, Sarita called again. Why don't you call her back?

Okay, okay I said, because ever since the auction I'd been wanting to tell Sarita about how hard Dad tried to buy that desk for her and how we actually almost had fun together that day. I guess I could at least ask her about the grieving teens support group. Because telling Liam about you did help. So maybe talking to others will help too. Who knows? It's worth a try. At least it doesn't feel impossible anymore and I can always quit if I don't like it. And hey, I could mention it to Liam and maybe he'll want to join too. You never know. But even if he doesn't, helping myself will help me to help him. Oh help. That sounds so pathetic.

And I must have said oh help out loud because Dazey jumped up and hugged me. She kind of got her hands caught in my fairy wings and said where on earth did you get those and I told her how I made them, and how when I was working on them I folded your quilt away and she said that's okay, sweetie, that's okay, I should have done that ages ago. And then we both just cried and cried and cried.

Then finally she said do you remember what I told you that time? I had to think a minute but then I knew what she meant. I had asked her once how to get over your death and she said I shouldn't think about getting over it because I never would, but that I could learn to live with it. I could find a way to tuck your memory into a tiny little pocket of my heart and then get on with my life.

I guess she should know.

And I guess I feel almost ready to do that now. So this might be the last time I write to you. But it won't be the last time I think of you. You do know that, don't you?

Next

After the Dead Babies' Birthday Party, Liam stops in at Gully's to pick up his books. Gully's left him a phone message saying that the prison is under control and he's coming home. He's on his way. That should be a relief, but Liam dreads facing him. And now he can't put it off much longer.

He goes to school to write his last two exams. The police are there questioning kids. They've set up an interview space in the library. They're taking kids in one by one. But of course they're not getting anywhere.

Nobody saw anything.

Nobody heard anything.

Nobody knows anything.

DDHS is buzzing with rumours though, because Youth and Crime have disappeared. Some kids say they've run away to Kingston. Some kids say Toronto. Others say no, they're hiding out at Youth's uncle's place in the country north of Dunlane. And still others say they've gone to Crime's grandmother's cottage.

There are a lot of rumours about what will happen next. Everyone wonders if Y4C will break up now, and if DumpLane's youth crime problem will be solved. But most expect it will only get worse over the summer because they've heard Y4C already has a new leader. The one thing everybody believes is that Ghoul Guy took over on Saturday night.

Liam isn't called down to the library for an interview. The teachers and principal still think he's a good kid. He wishes they would bring him in though. He'd confess to being Ghoul Guy in a minute. Because then they'd phone Gully and inform him what's his grandson is guilty of, so Liam won't have to.

He meets up with Harmony after their exams. "I talked to my mom," she says with a big smile. She's changed out of her fancy dress and lost the fairy wings. Now she looks like all the other girls, except she's way more beautiful. "And I guess I'm feeling a bit better about things."

"Man, wish I was." He's been psyching himself up for what comes next. "I gotta confess to Pete."

Her smile disappears. "Want me to come with?"

Does he ever. Everywhere, for the rest of his life. "Are you sure? I mean, considering, um, you know –"

"Please don't talk about it," she says. "Let's just go. Get it over with."

They find Pete in the trashed caretaker's office, trying to straighten up the disgusting mess. Liam hasn't told Harmony about Pete being his father, hasn't accepted it himself yet. It's still so shocking to suddenly have a dad. Part of him wishes he'd never found out. Too much information.

So he tries to act like Pete's just the cemetery caretaker. But he can tell that Pete knows he knows. They both keep staring at each other, but pretending they aren't. And Pete's way too eager to help Liam make things right.

Harmony doesn't say anything, just stands beside Liam, holding his hand. No, gripping his hand. Like she's reliving what Jordan/Youth did to her in this place.

"Thanks," he says when they're done. "Means a lot you were with me." He wants to say more, something to comfort her, but can't find the right words. So he just holds her, hoping she'll know how he feels.

She clings to him, pressing her face against his shoulder. He can feel her tears, warm on his neck. "You okay?" he says.

She shakes her head and snuffles, "Not really." Then she lets go and wipes her eyes with the back of her hand. "But I will be. What about you?"

"Better, but I still have to talk to Gully. And I need to face him on my own."

"Makes sense," she says. "See you later?"

"You bet." He walks Harmony to her door, then heads home.

When he gets there, Gully's out in the garden. He's kneeling down, tending his tomato plants with love. They've grown a lot since he and Liam planted them. Some have little yellow flowers already. Gully is so into his gardening that he doesn't even notice Liam standing there watching him.

"Need some help?" Liam finally says.

Gully leaps up, startled. Instantly on guard. "Oh hey," he says. "Sorry, didn't see you there. Still feeling a bit jumpy. Thanks for watering these for me."

"No problem." Yeah, right. What a suck-up. Showing Gully he's not all bad. At least he can be trusted with some things. "Gotta look after our killer tomatoes."

Gully gives a fake laugh. They've made this joke so many times, but it's not funny at the moment. Liam tries again. "So, you just get back?"

"Yup."

"Things okay at Millhaven now?"

"Probably be quiet for awhile." Gully looks exhausted from three days at the prison. "Maybe I'll even get some time off."

Liam's legs start shaking as he stands there. He shifts his weight to from one foot to the other, trying to control his nerves. Trying to look like he's not dancing. "That'd be good." If only Harmony was here to hold his hand, like she did while he talked to Pete.

But he can see his mom's face through the fog. More clearly than ever since she died. She's sitting on that beach log in her yellow raincoat, waving and smiling. Just for a minute. Then she disappears.

Gully's using a trowel to till the soil around the tomatoes. "So, how'd the exams go?" He keeps digging, careful and gentle.

"They're gone," Liam says. "Over. I think I did okay."

"Any summer plans?"

Oh yeah. His summer is all arranged. "You mean, like a job or something?" Ever since he came to Dunlane, Gully's been dropping hints about where he thinks Liam could work. Should work.

"That would be the idea."

Crunch time. "Actually, I'll be working for Pete."

"Working for Pete?" Gully says. "Doing what?"

"I, um, offered to work for free. Cleaning up around the cemetery, fixing the caretaker's office, cutting grass—whatever he wants."

Gully's shoulders shift and tighten as that sinks in. "He was okay with that?"

"Mostly. But he said the insurance won't cover everything. And some things can never be fixed. Some of the gravestones. Some of the maps and records that got destroyed are lost forever. That's unforgivable. But he'll let me do what I can."

"Ah." Liam can feel Gully figuring out that has to mean he was involved in the vandalism. "So I'm guessing that working for Pete isn't just about getting to know your father?"

"Not really. It's about making up for some bad stuff I did. But I guess getting to know him is a possibility." Not likely though. He's got Gully now. If he decides to get closer to a father figure, that's who he'll pick. Definitely.

Gully hands Liam some garden twine. "It's time to stake these plants," he says. "Can you cut me some of that?"

"Sure thing." Liam takes the ball of twine and starts snipping it into lengths with the garden shears. "I'll also be writing a letter of apology to the town for what happened. Saying I'm sorry for being disrespectful of the cemetery. For causing people so much pain. I'll send a copy to the newspaper too, so they can print it."

"Sounds like a good start," Gully takes a piece of twine from Liam. "But if you go public, the town will probably press charges."

"I've thought about that." Liam says. "I can handle it." He knows he deserves anything he gets. But he's hoping that since he's trying to make things right, if he's charged, the judge will consider community service.

Gully nods. "If you use twine," he says, "you have to be careful not to tie it too tight, or it will cut through the stalk." He tenderly ties a tomato plant to its stake. "So anyway," he says. "I stopped by the cemetery on my way home." He shakes his head. "Your mother and grandmother's stone. Covered with graffiti. Filthy, disgusting stuff. I can't believe anybody would do that."

Telling Gully is even harder than telling Harmony was. "Yeah. Well." Liam passes Gully another piece of twine. "I'm sorry you had to see that. I'll be the one cleaning it up. As soon as we're done here."

Gully keeps his head down for what feels like forever. Finally he says, "Will you be able to get it all off?"

"Pete thinks so. He says it's easier with new gravestones, because they're still shiny and polished."

"Right." Gully takes his time tying the next tomato plant to its stake. "You know, Liam." He turns and tips his gardening hat off his face. "Your mom was always her own person. *Always.* Everything she did, she wanted to do. I never had any influence over her choices. Don't think I didn't try." He tips his hat back down. "You need to understand that."

"I'm trying to." Liam cuts some more twine, way more than Gully could possibly need. "But it's hard, you know? It hurts so much."

"I know." Gully stakes another tomato plant. "Believe me, I know."

Liam offers him another piece of twine. "I'm sorry. I'm really, really sorry. For everything."

"I know that too," Gully says. "And it's okay." He finishes staking another tomato plant and points to the outdoor tap. "We're going to be okay."

"Yeah." Liam goes to fill the watering can for him. "Yeah, we are."

A huge thank you to everyone at Great Plains Teen Fiction for their enthusiastic response to this book, and to my gentle editor Anita Daher, for her brilliant insights, comments and suggestions. I'd also like to thank my husband Allan and my daughter Caitlin for their helpful advice on the manuscript, and the rest of my wonderful family for their constant support and inspiration.